HITTIN' LICKS FOR THE HOLIDAYS

Charleston

TRON HILL

URBAN AINT DEAD PRESENTS

URBAN AINT DEAD

P.O Box 448

Maybrook, NY 12543

No part of this book may be reproduced or transmitted in any form by any means electronic or mechanical, including photocopying, recording, or by any information storage system, without written permission from the publisher.

Copyright © 2025 By **Tron Hill**

All rights reserved. Published by URBAN AINT DEAD Publications.

Cover Design: P. Wise / The Wise Service

Edited By: Shawna Brim / Ladies of Lit

URBAN AINT DEAD and coinciding logo(s) are registered properties.

No patent liability is assumed with respect to the use of information contained herein. Although every precaution has been taken in the preparation of this book, the publisher and the author assume no responsibility for errors or omissions. Neither is any liability assumed for damages resulting from the use of the information contained herein. This is a work of fiction. Names, characters, places, and incidents are either the product of the author's imagination or are used fictitiously. Any resemblance to actual events, locales, or persons living or dead is entirely coincidental.

Contact Publisher at www.urbanaintdead.com

Email: urbanaintdead@gmail.com

Print ISBN: 978-1-969593-04-8

SOUNDTRACKS

Scan the QR Code below to listen to the Soundtracks/Singles of some of your favorite U.A.D titles:

Don't have Spotify or Apple Music?
No Sweat!
Visit your choice streaming platform and search URBAN AINT DEAD.

Currently on lock serving a bid?
JPay, iHeartRadio, WHATEVER!
We got you covered.
Simply log into your facility's kiosk or tablet, go to music and search
URBAN AINT DEAD.

URBAN AINT DEAD PRESENTS

Like & Follow us on social media:

FB - URBAN AINT DEAD

IG: @uadpresents

Tik Tok - @uadpresents

Submission Guidelines

Submit the first three chapters of your completed manuscript to urbanaintdead@gmail.com, subject line: Your book's title. The manuscript must be in a .doc file and sent as an attachment. The document should be in Times New Roman, double-spaced, and in size 12 font. Also, provide your synopsis and full contact information. If sending multiple submissions, they must each be in a separate email. Have a story but no way to submit it electronically? You can still submit to URBAN AINT DEAD. Send in the first three chapters, written or typed, of your completed manuscript to:

URBAN AINT DEAD
P.O Box 448
Maybrook, NY 12543

DO NOT send original manuscript. Must be a duplicate.
Provide your synopsis and a cover letter containing your full contact information.
Thanks for considering URBAN AINT DEAD.

CHAPTER ONE

The rhythm of the beat pulsated through his skull, every kick and snare syncing with the thud of his heartbeat. Eyes closed, he let the lyrics roam the interior of his mind — simple raw and unfiltered truths. They weren't just words; they were pieces of him torn from the cloth of his short seventeen years of life.

He exhaled slowly, leaving the last line to hang in the air like smoke.

From behind the glass, KG leaned forward in his chair. "You got sumn' else you wanna run ya mouth bout, lil nigga?" his voice cut through the hum of the booth headphones.

Shine remained silent a moment longer before opening his eyes. Through the glass, he caught the producer smirking at him, leaning over the mix board.

"Aye, you think I say 'nough?" Shine asked, before pulling the headphones off his ears.

"It ah 'nough – less you pay for more mix time, bubba."

KG leaned back in his chair, studying the young lyricist. The kid had talent – the kind that could take him far but only if he dug deep enough to find that extra fire inside of him. Right now, KG saw hunger, but not the kind that burned hot enough yet.

"Look ya, that's what big boi for." Shine smirked as he walked out of the booth and into the room. He sat on the black leather couch and stared at the mix board, thinking that finally his dream was about to become a reality —the only reality he saw fit for himself.

Since he was a snotty nose little boy running around the streets of Charleston, he'd fantasized about being a Lil Wayne or Lil Boosie, whom he regarded as the best in the game.

KG was still twisting the knobs on the board and pressing buttons when the studio door opened. The faint smell of cologne and smoke slipped in first – then came Big Mo.

Weighing in at two hundred and seventy pounds, Big Mo was a Charleston legend. For over two decades, he ran and supplied the streets with an iron fist that would make Suge Knight resemble a middle school bully. The stories of his reign traveled farther than the dope he moved – whispers about bodies that disappeared, corners that shifted overnight, and how one stare from him could freeze a whole block in place.

Some said he controlled the city's pulse. Others said he was the flatline — the violent cardiac arrest that stopped the street's heartbeat cold if he felt even the slightest disrespect.

His attire was a rich-casual – designer jeans, fresh sneakers, and a big tee that swallowed his thick frame. The heavy gold links resting on his chest matched the Rolex on his wrist, both screaming old money and street-earned respect. When he stepped into the booth, the air shifted like someone had opened a door to a different temperature.

Even KG, who wasn't impressed by much, sat up a little straight. There was something about Big Mo's presence – quiet, heavy – which made it seem like he carried the whole city's history on his shoulders and dared anyone to challenge it.

"Wassup, my nigga, Mo?" KG said, halfway standing to greet him.

Mo grinned, showing the kind of confidence that came with money and power. "Cain't even call it, my nigga. Sliding through, seein' what you and my boi been cooking up."

Shine stood, dapping him up out of respect. "Shid, you already know, Big Mo."

"Yeah, I hear you," Mo replied, eyeing the kid like he was sizing him up for something bigger than a handshake. "Lil nigga, ya getting betta e're time I hear you. I see dat you almost ready."

The corner of Shine's mouth inched upward as he began rubbing his palms together, which was out of habit. "Almost?"

Mo chuckled, deep and slow. "Yeah, almost. Come 'ere, lemme holla at you a sec."

He motioned toward the back office. Inside, the office smelled like success and too many secrets. Gold plaques covered the walls; some belonged to artists who were near burned out, others to those who'd vanished after one summer. Shine gratefully took it all in.

"Look ya, sit down," Mo said, lowering into his own chair. "Ain gon' keep you long."

Shine leaned forward, elbows on his knees. Mo's tone softened a bit, the way older cats did when they wanted you to listen.

"Ya know I knew your pops, right?" Mo began, "Ant was a solid dude. Never folded, even when life tried to break him. I always respected dat."

Shine nodded, keeping his eyes locked on him. "Yeah, Mama told me you use to hang together."

"More than just hung out," Mo said, tapping the desk. "We come up hustling long 'fore all this money. He had dreams too. You remind me of him – sharp, quiet, but you think too much 'fore you move. Dat a help you – and hurt you, depending on the room you in."

Shine didn't say anything. He'd learned at a young age that silence caused grown men to talk more.

Mo leaned back, interlocking his fingers. "Look ya, a few people already talking. You's got something. Ya ain't just another SoundCloud rapper. Ya real wit' it. I gon' bring ya under my wing – get you on the label, put you where ya s'posed to be, baby."

Shine exhaled, looking down at his shoes. "I preciate dat, Mo. Fo' real, my nigga. But I ain tryna rush nothing. I got school, ball… and my ma be on me heavy bout finishing it."

Mo let out a low laugh, not mockingly but like he'd heard that before. "School gon' always be dere, Shine. But time and opportunity ain't. Shid, you act like dat shit alone gon' take ya beyond yonder."

"I know," Shine said carefully. "But I can't drop out and leave her hanging. Pops gone. I gotta be the one to make sure she straight and happy. Plus, if I do this, I gotta do it right. Can't get tricked like half dem rappers don' sign they life away fo' a chain and a lil advance."

Mo raised an eyebrow, amused. "I see ya been doing the home-work, but ya think I – I do you like dat?"

"Hell nah," Shine said, his voice calm but firm.

Mo leaned forward again, tapping two fingers against the desk. "I respect dat you smart. Just don't go thinkin' yourself outta your own blessin', ya feel me?"

That line hung in the air a second, encircling Shine as if it was mere amusement, but it carried something heavier underneath. Mo smiled like he already knew the next few moves on the board.

"But sayless," Mo said, standing, "think on it. But don't think too long. De world ain't waitin' on nobody."

Shine stood up, dapping him. "I already know, and I got you."

"Ight," Mo said, giving him a half-smile that didn't quite reach his eyes. "Keep that hunger. I can do sumn' with that."

Outside, the studio lights hit Shine's face differently. He displayed an expression caught between pride and uncertainty. KG looked over from across the room like, *What was that about?*

Shine just nodded and smirked before he grabbed his bag and stepped out into Charleston's cool winter breeze.

The sky was fading into that late-evening purple, the kind that made the city glow in uniqueness. Catching the transit bus at the corner, he put his earphones in, taking a seat at the very back.

As the bus pulled off, Shine leaned back against the cracked seat and stared out the window. Mo's words echoed quietly inside his head – *don't think yourself outta your own blessing.*

He didn't know what Mo really meant by that, but something in the way he said it made Shine's palms itch again.

The bus rumbled down Meeting Street, the city sliding by in blurry streaks of headlights and neon reflections. Shine kept replaying Mo's words, trying to decode the weight behind them. *Don't think yourself outta your own blessing.*

He couldn't tell if Mo was motivating him… or warning him.

His stop dinged.

Shine stood, tugging his hoodie tighter as the doors hissed open. The cold Charleston air immediately wrapped around him. The Gullah Geechee neighborhood was as usual. Kids were still running around outside, music still echoed from cracked windows, and then there was the continuous porch activity of drugs being sold.

Crossing the courtyard, he spotted T-Man trekking across grass, a tall shadowy figure under the flickering streetlight, dressed in his usual hoodie and fitted jeans.

"My nigga, wussup, cus?" Shine called out.

T-Man broke into a grin, adjusting his glasses, before dapping him up with a heavy slap. "Shine! What up wit' it, my nigga? Where you been at, boi?"

"You already know – the studio," Shine said with a smirk. "Tryna make this rap shit happen for real."

"I'm telling ya ain't nothing wrong with that," T-Man replied. "Ain't shit been going on out here but the same-ol-same."

T-Man paused then snorted. "Nah, lemme stop lying. Bruh, tell me why dem boi, Reek and Lil Duno, got to boxing earlier?"

Shine raised his eyebrows. "For real? Bout what?"

"Some dumb shit," T-Man chuckled. "Nigga, Reek say Duno owe him fifteen dollars from two weeks back – fifteen damn dollars, bro."

He reenacted the fight, arms flailing, glasses sliding down his nose a bit. "Reek swung like he was mad at the air. Da boi missed every punch. Duno caught him wit' one lil tap – *bah!* – an' Reek folded like laundry."

Shine doubled over laughing, nearly losing his breath. "Aw, hell nah, not Reek. The boi swear he Mayweather."

"Mayweather my ass," T-Man said. "Da boi more like May-feather. Light as hell in da ass."

They laughed again, their voices loud enough to ricochet between the houses.

"Aye," T-Man said, wiping his eyes, "ya tryna slide through The Pad? Niggas gon' be over dere deep tonight."

"I wit' that, my nigga," Shine said. "Lemme hit the crib first though."

"Sayless. Me swing back through in bout twenty."

They dapped up and split ways. T-Man walked off toward the cut behind one of the houses, still chuckling to himself.

Shine headed toward his own home but slowed when he saw two people stepping out of the front door. A white man and woman, both were dressed like they'd walked out of some corporate meeting. Suits and briefcases in hand. The pair was out of place in every possible way.

He arched an eyebrow, watching them move quickly to their car. The woman glanced back once as they climbed in, like she was checking something off in her head. The engine rumbled to life, and they drove off as if the whole experience was already behind them.

He watched until their taillights disappeared, unease creeping into his stomach. Something didn't sit right. He couldn't remember the last time he'd seen white people leave from his house.

Heading inside, the aromatic smell of cooking food drifted through the hallway and into his nostrils.

"Ma!" he called out, dropping his coat and bag on the couch.

"Yeah, I'm in the kitchen!" she answered.

Shine walked toward the sound of her voice, feeling a light shift in the house's energy – like something had happened before he got home.

Stepping into the kitchen, Shine walked up beside his mother as she stood over the sink, sleeves pushed up, suds sliding down her forearms. He leaned in and kissed her cheek then propped himself back against the counter, arms folded. Out of the corner of his eye, he caught a stack of papers on the kitchen table – white pages slapped with bold red ink.

He didn't say anything about it – yet. "Who dem people just left?"

His mother paused, staring out the window like she was replaying the moment. "No one but the bank."

"Wha' they want?"

She let out a dry laugh, but it didn't sound amused at all. "The same thing everybody want… some money folks ain't got."

Shine's jaw flexed. "Some money? How much?"

"An amount you don't need to worry bout." She flicked her hand dismissively. "Now, how was your day?"

Shine twisted his lips, shrugging one shoulder. "It was aight."

He hesitated. He already knew how she felt about the whole rap thing. She thought it was a distraction, a trap disguised as a dream. Still, he took a breath. "Big Mo done offered me a contract."

His mother froze mid-dish rinse, water running over her hands. She turned just enough to look at him.

"And yuh tell him wha'?"

Shine pushed off the counter and walked over to the table, his fingers hovering over the papers. "I told him I gon' think bout it… cause I got school and ball."

She went back to scrubbing, her movements sharper now. "Exactly, you ain't got no business getting caught up in all that right now, Shine. Baby, you too close. You got a future sitting right in front of you. School, that diploma, and football – you keep your mind on that. These streets, and that rap game, don't love nobody, and a contract don't mean you safe. It mean control wit' all eyes on you. Then come the pressure and the temptation."

She rinsed a plate, setting it in the rack. "You start chasing short-cuts, you gon' lose the long game. I ain't raise you to gamble every-thing for a microphone and a maybe."

Shine didn't argue. He just let her words wash over the room.

His gaze dropped back to the table. He reached out and picked up one of the papers. Red letters in bold font. FINAL NOTICE.

His throat tightened.

Behind him, his mother suddenly stopped washing dishes – like she could sense exactly which paper he'd picked up. Hell, it was on the very top, something she now regretted.

The kitchen went quiet, thick with something unsaid.

Shine's eyes moved slowly over the paper, every line tightening something in his chest. He swallowed.

"Ma… they…"

She cut him off before he could finish. "I done told you you don't need to worry 'bout that. I'ma figure it out."

"But…"

Her voice snapped like a twig under pressure. "Shine. Mind your own."

She reached out and snatched the paper from his hand with a quick, frustrated swipe, folding it sharply as if the creases could hide the truth.

Before the tension could thicken any further, small footsteps pattered into the room.

Angela, the youngest in the house, all bright eyes and messy braids, practically bounced toward him, energy spilling over like sunlight in motion.

"Shiinnee!"

She threw her arms around his waist, squeezing tight. Shine forced a smile and hugged her back, tapping the top of her head.

Their mother exhaled through her nose, smoothing her work apron.

"Angela, you done finish your homework yet?"

Angela groaned. "Yep, I did all of it."

"Good. And y'all—" her eyes flicked between Shine and her little angel, "clear out my kitchen while I finish wit' this dinner. Go'on out my way."

Shine patted Angela's back, guiding her out, as their mother turned back toward the stove, shoulders stiff, the folded notice still gripped tight in her hand.

CHAPTER TWO

The night was cool, though not too cold yet. The wind was blowing just enough wind to rattle the palmetto leaves above the parking lot. Shine sat posted on the hood of T-Man's old burgundy Crown Vic, legs stretched out, hoodie hanging over his shoulders. A small crowd of neighborhood heads floated around – laughing and talking trash, as music thumped from somebody's Bluetooth speaker.

Shine wasn't saying much, just vibing and watching. That was what he did mostly, especially when he was in his thoughts.

A few minutes passed before Roscoe came strolling up, jeans sagging, with his dreads tied back by a bandana. He threw his hand out.

"Wassup, my nigga?" Roscoe said.

Shine hopped off the hood just enough to dap him, pulling him in quick. "Cooling. Boy, ya flam ass look like ya been digging through the trash again."

Roscoe smirked. "Ya mama," he shot back, and a couple dudes nearby snickered.

Shine shrugged. "At least she got her own trash to dig through. You all in somebody else's shit, jokey."

That got a louder laugh.

Roscoe held his chest dramatically. "Look ya, aight, ya got dat." He leaned back against the car next to Shine. After a second, his face shifted — the humor draining into something dead serious. "But look… lemme talk to you fuh ah minute."

Shine arched an eyebrow. "What gwan?"

Roscoe scratched the back of his head, eyes darting around. "Lemme hol' sumn', bruh."

Shine tilted his head. "Ya need it?"

"Hell yeah I need dat bad." Roscoe's expression appeared almost offended. "I'm all gone – messed up right now. Ya know how it go."

Shine shook his head slowly, almost disappointed.

"Nah. I don't know how it go… cause I do what I got do to keep what I need. So I ain't gotta be out here asking for nuthin'. Like some folks."

The entire group went quiet for a second – one of those moments when the air got still enough to hear your own heartbeat.

Roscoe stared at him, lips pursed, jaw tight. Then, he jabbed a finger into Shine's chest.

"Aye, nigga… every dog got he day. And right now, it mine. But it ain't gone be for long."

Shine didn't even flinch. "Ya, it will… if you keep worrying bout dog days instead of getting' on up. Look at how you doing right now."

For a moment, it looked like Roscoe might swing at him. Instead, he burst into a ridiculous laugh.

"Oooh, dis nigga tink he up cause he poppin' his lil mess!" He chuckled, looking around at the others for backup. "Quarter pound ass boy right deh."

A few people cracked up, but most of them just glanced between the two, entertained.

Shine smirked, leaning back on the hood like the whole moment didn't faze him. He was used to Roscoe yapping when a nigga turned him down. Some of the stuff he said, some would take as him hating or even take it personal, but Shine had known him since kindergarten. He was just being him – the typical asshole.

"Ya, it a lil gas, but it more than what ya got. Period, flam boy…" Shine shrugged his shoulders, glancing around.

Shine looked over the lot again – the busted streetlights, the peeling paint on some of the houses, the same dudes posted in the same spots they'd been in since he was ten. All this noise, all this movement, and he still felt that pressure in his chest from the bank papers sitting on the kitchen table, which none of these could take his mind away from. His family had to escape this life.

Chump change. That was all the lil pound he'd been flipping was – enough to keep his pockets warm though not enough to stop the eviction notice that was practically screaming at his mama.

He sucked his teeth and exhaled. His mind was spinning with numbers, options, impossibilities.

Before he could finish the thought, T-Man slapped his hands together. "Aye, you tryna slide through The Pad fuh a minute?" he asked, nodding toward his car.

Shine pushed off the hood. "Ya, let's ride."

They were halfway in when the back door snatched open. Roscoe hopped in like he belonged there.

T-Man didn't even turn his head. "Aye, boi, yee don't need to be gettin' in if you ain got no money."

Roscoe leaned forward, offended. "Man, dat what homeboys fo', and y'all niggas got me messed up if you think I'ma just be standing out here looking brokey."

T-Man rolled his eyes so hard it looked painful. "Mannnnn, he flam… boi, ya is brokey."

He shot a look across the car at Shine like, *Your turn, bruh.*

Shine rubbed his forehead and shook his head slowly. "Man… I got you this time, aight? Lawd, this getting old."

Roscoe sat back with his arms folded like he'd won something, while mumbling to himself.

T-Man started the car, muttering, "Yo ass betta not start mouthin' like you important or some shit, or I'ma kick yo' ass out."

The Crown Vic rattled as it pulled out of the lot, headlights sweeping across the cracked pavement.

Twenty minutes later, they turned into a dimly lit strip on the Eastside. The car rolled to a stop in front of The Pad, the old club spot where everybody in the hood came to smoke, gamble, argue, flex, or kill some time before they went home to whatever mess waited on them.

Shine could see that The Pad was jumping tonight. Music was spilling out the doors, neon lights flickering on chrome rims, people laughing, smoking, arguing, the whole block breathing heavy with Thursday night energy. T-Man pulled the car around the lot into a dirt spot between two old but clean cars. The engine knocked once before it died.

The trio hopped out, pulling their hoods up to protect against the cool breeze as they moved toward the entrance.

Before they could even get to the door, Shine spotted Cuttty, Big Mo's right-hand man, posted up with a thick gold chain and a cup in his hand. The other hand was on the waist of a local baddie. Cuttty saw him too and broke into a wide grin.

"Wassup, lil nigga?" Cuttty called, reaching out for a dap. "Wha ya got goin' on?"

Shine dapped him and smirked. "Nuthin' much. Out here wit' my niggas, tryna find sumn' to mash on."

Cuttty laughed hard. "I know dat right. Shiiiid… it's just three a y'all? Man, pull up VIP wit' me an' my people."

Shine glanced at T-Man, who raised his eyebrows like, *Nigga, ya the one he talking to*. Shine scratched his head, leaning closer to Cuttty.

"Cutty, a nigga pockets ain right fuh all that," he muttered lowly.

Cuttty sucked his teeth. "Nigga, dis on me. Fa real. C'mon, stoppuh playing. Let we do dis, yah?"

Shine nodded and motioned for the other two to follow.

Cuttty's entourage pushed through the crowd like they owned the place – two heavyset dudes flanked them, a group of fine girls trailing behind, all giggles and perfume. They moved through the bodies swaying to bass-heavy music, stepping over spilled drinks and weaving past mugging dudes posted on the wall.

When they got to VIP, the security rope dropped like magic.

Bottles of champagne hit the table almost immediately, cold and sweating. One of Cuttty's girls, brown-skinned with locs trailing down her back, slid right in between Shine and T-Man like she belonged there.

Everybody was talking loud, laughing, snapping pictures and recording videos. Roscoe damn near melted into the couch, eyes wide like he couldn't believe he was breathing VIP air.

Up front, the DJ hyped the crowd while everyone waited for somebody to finally take the stage. Then a local rapper hopped up, pushing out one of his singles. The beat slapped, and his chopped-up lyrics had a few heads nodding, a couple folks mumbling along—but that was about it. The room never lifted.

It wasn't the turnt-up moment he pictured himself owning.

Cuttty watched the rapper with a blank, and unimpressed stare. Then, his eyes slid sideways toward Shine.

He leaned toward one of the dudes beside him and whispered something in his ear. The dude nodded and got up immediately, weaving through the crowd toward the DJ booth.

Cuttty leaned closer to Shine, grinning.

"Lil one," he said, tapping Shine's leg, "you tryna get up dere an' tek dis nigga place?"

Shine froze, staring at him. "Huh?"

Cuttty nodded toward the stage. "Boi, you done heard me. Nigga, you tryna get up dere or wha?"

Shine hesitated, chest tightening until it felt hard to breathe. He'd never performed in front of anybody outside the studio. Never spit a verse without a booth, a mic, and a glass pane to hide behind. Now there was nothing between him and the world. He looked at the stage again – the lights glaring down, the eyes waiting, the whole damn club leaning in like they were expecting something better.

"Shid," Shine said slowly, "I ain't even got no track fa them to play fuh me."

Cuttty cut his eyes at him. "Nigga… ya tryna get up dere or nah?"

Shine shrugged like it wasn't a big deal, even though his palms were sweating.

Then, the rapper finished his set. The DJ's voice blasted through the speakers.

"Aiiight now, nex' up, one dem Charleston's young thoroughbred bout ta hit the stage wit' his single called *Affiliated*… turn up for muthafuckin' *Shine G!*"

Heads turned as the crowd looked for a person they had never heard of. Cuttty smiled. T-Man looked shocked. Roscoe's mouth fell open.

Shine's heart thudded once, loud as a beat on a drum. He couldn't believe this was happening. He hadn't prepared himself to be in front of a few hundred people, tonight. Then, he looked over at T-Man. A semi-scapegoat formed in his mind.

Shine pushed up from the couch, clearing his throat. "Aye, Cutty… dat the only track you got here?"

Cutty shook his head, scrolling through his phone. "Naah, li'l bro. I got dem ten dat finished an' mixed, duh CD KG couldn't keep he damn mouth shut 'bout."

Shine nodded, decision landing fast. His nerves were crawling, but he wasn't about to fold in front of all these people. He jerked his head at T-Man. "Aye, come on wit' me."

T-Man's eyes widened; he was just as unprepared as Shine. But without a word, he stood. If Shine was going, he was going too. That was day-one loyalty.

They pushed through the crowd, slipping past shoulders and phones and over the heavy bass rattling the floor. When they reached the stage, Shine leaned in close to the DJ, "It ah different track. Me and my partner gon' do *Vert*."

The DJ shot him a curious look then smirked and grabbed the mic.

"Aight, Charleston, dem switchin' it up – say dem got somethin' even betta fa y'all!"

The crowd looked on in anticipation.

The beat for *Vert* dropped – thick, rhythmic, and bouncing – and Shine felt the fear melt right out his bones. Him and T-Man slid into their first verses like they'd been rehearsing them all week.

The crowd ate it up – drinks were in hands spilling, people shouting, heads nodding hard. By the time they hit the hook, the whole spot was turning up.

They finished with a final punchline that set the crowd off again.

Cutty was waiting at the steps, face lit up with pride. He dapped them both up hard. "Dat's wha' the fuck I talking 'bout, fa real."

Shine smiled, adrenaline still buzzing through him. T-Man was out of breath but grinning wide. The three of them headed back toward their section where bottles were already being cracked open. The night was warming up around them like the start of something big.

CHAPTER THREE

Shine's alarm clock went off like a hammer to his skull.

He groaned, eyes still glued shut. His head pounded like the drums of a war cry. They were the thunderous echoes from the night before at The Pad. His mother had already left for work – her car wasn't in the driveway – and the quiet house only made the throb in his head feel louder. He pushed himself up and staggered toward the bathroom, swallowed two Tylenols dry, and leaned on the sink as the medicine slid down.

Pasting his tooth brush, he shuffled down the hallway toward Angela's room.

"Aye… Angie. Get up," he grumbled around the handle jutting from his mouth.

She didn't move.

Shine frowned, stepped closer, and reached under her blanket, grabbing her foot. With a quick pull, he yanked her right off the mattress and onto the floor.

"School time," he said, toothpaste flying from his lip.

"Mannnn…" Angela groaned, wiping her eyes with the back of her hand.

Shine shook his head and walked off, still brushing as he headed back to his room to put on his clothes.

A few minutes later, he was in the kitchen, hoodie halfway on his head, fixing them both bowls of cereal. Angela came in slow, dragging her feet, one hand pressed against her forehead.

"My head hurt…" she muttered lowly.

Shine didn't even look up at first. "Aye, gal, you gon' have to tough it out like da strong lil' man ya be."

Her face scrunched. "I ain't no man."

"Whatever. Just eat," Shine uttered, scrolling through his phone as he leaned against the counter, spoon halfway in his mouth.

Angela sat down… but she didn't touch the food. She stared at it. First, her eyelids began to flutter, then her breathing became off, shallow and shaky. Shine hadn't noticed.

Not until she picked up the bowl. Angela was going to dump it, but her knees buckled.

The bowl crashed. Milk splashed. Angela's small body crumbled to the floor.

Shine's phone slipped right out his hand as he spun. "ANGELA!"

He slid to the floor, scooping her up, panic exploding in his chest. She wasn't responding. Her head lolled to the side. Shine shook her, voice cracking, as he shouted her name again. *Where was his phone?*

Everything after that was a blur – the ambulance, the sirens, him following the medics as they carried his sister into the back of it. His mind was so scrambled and confused that he'd almost forgot to call his mother before they arrived at MUSC Shawn Jenkins Children's Hospital.

Hours later, Shine and his mother stood at Angela's bedside in the children's hospital in Charleston.

The ICU room was too quiet, except for the steady mechanical beeping echoing through the cold air. Angela's small body lay beneath the covers, her hair pushed aside where the nurses had placed sensors along her scalp. Tubes curled from her mouth and nose. The rise and fall of her chest wasn't on her own; it was the ventilator helping her breathe.

Shine stood on one side of the bed with his hand wrapped around hers. His mother stood on the other side, shoulders trembling, her lips pressed together to stop the sobs. Tears streaked her cheeks in every way.

"Baby girl…" she whispered, brushing Angela's forehead. "Mama's right here. I right here, baby…"

Shine swallowed hard, blinking fast. He leaned down close to his sister's ear. "Ya ain't leaving us, Angie. Ya hear me? Ya ain't…"

The door clicked open.

Dr. Mason stepped inside with a nurse trailing behind him. His coat was wrinkled, his face tired and pale. He cleared his throat softly.

"Mrs. Mathis… I need to speak with you," he said. "In my office please."

Shine looked at Angela one more time before letting go of her hand.

He and his mother followed the doctor down a long hallway. To him, each light they passed under felt a little too bright, every sound a bit too sharp.

The doctor closed the door behind them and motioned for them to sit. Papers, scans, and a half-finished cup of coffee cluttered his desk. He pushed them aside with a shaky hand.

"First—" Doctor Mason began, "I want to tell you that your daughter is stable – for now. But her condition is extremely serious."

Shine leaned forward. "Serious? How serious? She been jus' fine this morning."

Doctor Mason pulled up a scan on the medical imaging monitor for them to see. A bright, white bloom showed inside the shape of Angela's brain.

"She suffered a ruptured cerebral aneurysm. Basically, a small vessel in the brain ballooned and then burst. The bleeding caused her to collapse, and the pressure from the blood forced her into a coma."

Shine's mother covered her mouth as tears started falling again.

"Now," the doctor continued, "this isn't a routine aneurysm. The rupture is located deep near the brainstem – an area extremely difficult to access. It's what we call a rare basilar apex rupture."

He paused. "And I'll be honest… Only one surgeon in this region has the experience and training to perform the procedure she needs. His name is Dr. Marcus Hale. He's the chief cerebrovascular surgeon at Saint Augustine NeuroCenter."

Shine frowned. "Only one doctor?"

"Yes," Doctor Mason said, nodding. "Angela's case is... well, it's not something most neurosurgeons will attempt. The vessel involved is fragile. The location is dangerous. It requires an emergency craniotomy for aneurysm clipping."

He saw their confusion and explained further.

"We would have to open a portion of her skull," he said slowly, "locate the ruptured artery deep in her brain, and place a titanium clip across it to stop the bleeding. Then, we'd relieve the pressure that's already building inside her skull. If we don't... if we delay..." His voice dipped low. "The pressure could cause a permanent, irreversible coma. Or... death."

Shine's mother wiped at her face with a shaking hand. "Then do whateva ya got to do," she blurted out quickly. "Get that docta. Get whoeva ya need. Jes' save my baby."

Doctor Mason shifted in his seat. He looked away for a moment, exhaling heavily.

"There's... something else," he began to explain. "Dr. Hale operates out of a private facility. He doesn't accept county guarantees, and he requires full payment upfront before he mobilizes his team and books the hybrid operating room."

Shine straightened, eyes narrowing. "Wha' ya tryna say?"

The doctor swallowed. "For Dr. Hale to take her case, the hospital will need a guarantee of three hundred and twenty thousand dollars before the surgery can proceed."

Shine and his mother froze.

"Three... three hundred and..." She couldn't even finish. Her voice broke.

The nurse looked down. Dr. Mason continued, seeming almost apologetic.

"The equipment he uses, the hybrid OR, the titanium clips, the specialized staff – it's all extremely costly. And with a case this rare... he can not begin without the payment in full."

Silence filled the room like smoke. Shine's heart hammered so hard he felt dizzy. Three hundred and twenty thousand dollars.

The doctor leaned forward, his voice heavy. "I wish I had better news or even a better option. But if we don't secure Doctor Hale soon… Angela won't survive another bleed."

Shine stood up slowly, jaw trembling, hands balled into fists. He looked at his mother, who was close to crumbling in the chair. He looked back at the doctor, who couldn't meet his gaze. Then, he thought of Angela laying in that bed and the machines keeping her alive.

"Okay," his mother whispered, voice low but certain. "I'ma get it."

Dr. Mason blinked. "Ma'am… this is a tremendous amount of money…"

"I say, I get it," his mother repeated, fire rising behind her tears. "Whateva I got ta do."

Shine and his mother walked out of the office before the doctor could say another word.

The hallway felt colder. The beeping machines echoed louder. And every step he took pulled him closer to a decision he couldn't turn back from.

CHAPTER FOUR

The elevator doors slid open, and Shine followed behind his mother, both moving like their world was on the verge of falling apart. Neither had said a word since leaving Doctor Mason's office. The doctor's voice kept replaying in Shine's head – *ruptured aneurysm… skull opened… titanium clip… three hundred twenty thousand dollars… pay in full.*

His stomach wouldn't stop twisting.

After they'd made it to his mother's insurance agency, both hurriedly stepped inside. Fluorescent lights buzzed loud enough to irk Shine's nerves. His mother walked up to the counter, voice shaky but still trying to keep it together.

"Hi… Ah-I need ta talk to someone 'bout my daughter. She—she need a emergency surgery."

The woman at the desk gave her one of those fake professional smiles. "Of course, ma'am. Do you have your policy number?"

His mother nodded, digging through her purse with trembling fingers. Shine watched her struggle, and it made heat creep up his neck. She finally handed the card over, and the woman typed slow as hell, like she had all day.

After a minute, she said, "Okay… you can step into office three. Miss Parker will assist you."

They walked into a little room with beige walls and a desk that looked too neat, like an office where nobody did real work. A middle-aged woman with glasses sat behind the metal desk, giving them that rehearsed, '*I understand*', look.

"Mrs. Mathis, how can we help you today?"

His mother broke before she even got the words out. "My daughter… she collapsed this morning. The docta say she had a ruptured an-aneurysm. She… she need a emergency surgery by some private docta. They gon' have to open her skull." Then her voice cracked. "I just need ta know can my insurance cover it."

Miss Parker typed for what felt like hours. She squinted at the screen, then sighed.

"I'm… very sorry. But under your policy – due to the downgraded plan you switched to last year – we cannot cover this specific procedure."

Shine blinked slowly. "Wha' you mean y'all cain't cover it?"

Miss Parker kept going like she didn't hear the edge creeping into his voice.

"There are exclusions on certain neurological surgeries, and because the operation needs to be done by a specialized, out-of-network, surgeon, the claim will be denied."

His mother leaned forward. "Denied? My baby is in a coma. She— she could die. Ya–ya telling me y'all cain't help us?"

Miss Parker folded her hands. "I wish there was something I could do. But based on the policy you selected, we…"

Shine exploded.

"Man, get the hell outta heah with dat policy shit!" he snapped, slamming his hand on the desk so hard that her cup of pens were now rolling across the desk. "Ya sittin' heah talking like dis ain't somebody's damn life!"

Ms. Parker stiffened. "Sir, I need you to calm down…"

"Cal'm down?" Shine shoved her computer monitor aside, sending papers flying, as well with it. "My sista in da hospital fightin' fo' her life, and you tell us some technical bullshit?"

"Shine!" his mother screamed, grabbing his arm.

He kicked the trashcan over, sending it crashing against the wall. The lady jumped back like he was about to jump across the desk.

"Sir, I'm calling security…"

His mother wrapped both arms around him, pulling him toward the door. "Shine, baby come on. Please. Please!"

He let her drag him out, chest heaving, veins thrumming with rage, his throat tightening so much it was hard to swallow.

They made it to the parking lot before his mother broke. She leaned against the car, face buried in her hands, sobbing so hard her whole body trembled.

Shine's anger melted the second he saw her like that.

"Ma…" He pulled her in, arms tight around her, resting his chin on the top of her head as her tears soaked through his shirt.

"They—they just gon' let ha' die," she cried. "My baby… my baby girl. I don' know what ta do. I don' know what ta do…"

Shine felt his own tears slipping, hot and silent. He tried to blink them back, but they kept falling.

"Weh gon' figure it out," he whispered, voice thick and breaking. "I swear fo' God. Ma, I don' care what I got ta do. I don' care who I got ta talk to or how far I got ta go…" He tightened his hold on her. "I ain't lettin' Angela die. I promise you dat."

His mother shook against him, but she clung to his shirt like she believed him… like that was the only thing she could do… believe.

And right there, in that cold parking lot, with both of them crying under a gray Charleston sky, something inside Shine snapped into place.

Whatever lines he thought he'd never cross? They didn't exist anymore.

CHAPTER FIVE

Shine sat in the passenger's seat, hands gripping his denim pants, like they could squeeze them into sheds. T-Man sat beside him, quiet, watching as streaks of tears ran down his homeboy's face. His chest rose and fell in uneven gasps. Shine's mind was spinning in over drive. Doctor's Mason and Hale, the hospital, the insurance denial… the impossible $320,000.

The car door opened, and Blow hopped in, snapping Shine out of his thoughts. Sliding across the backseat, he gave Shine's shoulder a little shake. Blow, like T-Man, was one of Shine's closest homeboys.

Standing at 5'11", Blow was of a dark-brown complexion and on the pudgy side of life. Yet, he was one of the flyest niggas Shine knew. The man stayed clean and was always on a hustle. No matter what the risk was, if money was involved, he was only a few feet away.

"Damn, my boi… I heard 'bout Angela," Blow said, shaking his head slowly. "I know dat shit ain easy fa you, my nigga."

Shine blinked, continuing to stare straight ahead.

"Look," Blow continued, leaning forward, voice low but steady. "Whateva we gotta do… it gon' get done, my nigga. I'm ridin' witchu."

Shine blinked back another tear as Blow's words sank in.

"Matter fact," Blow said, "fore I left, I had sumn' I been cookin' up… An' I know fa sho' it some racks in dat bihh."

Shine wiped at the streaks running down his face with the back of his hand. "Blow… dem folks want tree hunnid and twenty," he said, voice breaking just enough to make the words feel heavier.

Blow froze for a second. "Wha ya mean… three twenty?" He sat back in disbelief, shaking his head slowly. "Thousand? Three hunnid an' twenty thousand? Damn…"

Shine just stared out the window, silence stretching between them. T-Man's eyes flicked between the two, both unsure of what to say. The streetlights casted long, fractured shadows in the car.

Finally, Shine whispered, his voice tight. "But shid… anything ah start."

The car stayed quiet for a beat longer as Shine was partly consumed by heavy thoughts. Then, Blow began to rub the hair of his chin. "Ya know Draco an' his crew be clockin' like a fifty ball. One my lil' hoes be fuckin' wit da nigga off an' on. Her name Chelsea; she from roun' dey way, say dem niggas be stashin' da money at a spot ova on Claybourne. Shiid, my nigga, I check it out tonight, den tomorrow, weh crash it. She say it don' be nothin' but like two niggas in dey, an' Draco one of 'em, so dat definitely sweet—"

T-Man cut him off. "Ain't nuthin' sweet less it's done an' handled."

"Nigga, ya know what I mean," Blow said, already knowing T-Man was always the critical thinker when it came to pulling a move. "Matta fact, leh slide through dey now an' peep game. Den you tell me if it sweet or not."

T-Man glanced over at Shine, who wasn't even in the car mentally. He was still staring straight past the windshield, jaw set, eyes glassy – lost somewhere dark. T-Man could only imagine what was tearing him up on the inside. He didn't have a little sister, but if it had been one of his nieces, he'd be the same way if not worse.

"Ya tryna do that?" T-Man asked, keeping his eyes on Shine.

When Shine didn't answer, T-Man reached over and tapped him on the arm – hard enough to snap him back.

"Ya tryna do that?" T-Man asked again.

Shine blinked, breath shaky. He dragged a hand across his face and pinched the bridge of his nose like he was holding back a migraine – or a breakdown.

"Yeah… whateva," he muttered, voice low and drained. Shine hadn't heard a thing they'd said. All he could see was Angela – her little body limp on the floor, her lips losing color, the way her head rolled when he tried to shake her awake. The sound of her hitting the ground kept replaying in his skull like a broken track.

He kept wondering if he could've done something different… If he hadn't gone out the night before… If he'd just checked on her sooner when she made mention of the headache. Every "what if" stacked on his chest like bricks, making it hard to breathe.

Shakingly, Shine reached to let the window down. It felt as if he was suffocating.

"Ya good, boi?" T-Man watched his fidgeting fingers attempt to let the window down. He hated seeing his homie like this, and he was just as ready as Shine was to get that money.

Turning over the ignition, T-Man put the car in drive to give Shine whatever air he needed.

CHAPTER SIX

The next day, Shine stood in the studio booth with the headphones hanging crooked over his ears. He tried to focus on the beat thumping through the speakers – tried to let the music drown out the mess in his head – but nothing was doing the job. Every time he opened his mouth, the words tangled themselves up, coming out sloppy, and offbeat.

KG tapped the glass again, shaking his head, as he hit the spacebar. The beat stopped abruptly.

"Aight, from da top," KG said, trying to keep the irritation out of his voice, though he was on his third restart.

Shine inhaled and tried again. But halfway through the first bar, his voice cracked. He couldn't keep the picture of Angela out of his mind – her still body, the machines, the doctor's voice echoing that number he couldn't afford.

He stumbled — again.

"Damn!" he yanked the headphones off and slammed them against the booth chair. His chest heaved hard, heat racing through him like anger was the only thing holding him together.

KG, Big Mo, and two other dudes stood on the other side of the glass, watching. Even through the soundproofing, Shine could almost hear their thoughts.

He pushed out the booth, heading for the studio's exit door with his jaw clenched and fists balled. But before he could make it out, a heavy hand gripped his shoulder.

Big Mo.

The man didn't say a word. He didn't have to. One look at Shine's eyes – the glaze, the swelling, the way he couldn't hold focus – told Mo everything he needed to know.

"Come holla at me in da office," Mo said quietly.

A single tear slipped past Shine's control as he nodded and followed Mo down the hallway. His breathing felt uneven, shaky. He sank into the chair across from Mo's desk as if the weight of life had knocked the bones out of him.

Mo sat down slowly, studying Shine like a father trying to read a son who'd finally reached his breaking point.

"Wha' going on, family?" Mo asked.

Shine opened his mouth, closed it, then shook his head. His throat burned. His chest continued to heave. Another tear rolled down his face, dropping onto his jean leg.

Finally, he managed to say something, even though his voice was cracking. "My sista… she on da verge of dyin', man. Da muthafuckin' docta talkin' 'bout three hunnid and twenty thousand fo' her surgery. Three twenty. Where da fuck we s'posed ta get dat?"

He dropped his head, staring at the floor. He didn't want Mo to see him crying, but at the same time, he didn't care anymore. His little sister was slipping away, and every piece of his pride was falling with her.

After a long moment, Shine wiped his face and forced out, "If I sign… how much you gon' give me off top?"

Mo leaned back, looking him dead in the eyes, no flinching, no sugarcoating.

"I cain't give you that much," he said straight. "But let me peep da contract again."

He tapped the desk, thinking. His tone softened.

"You my lil mans. But listen, whatever way you get that money, you gon' to need a legit source to send it from, especially fo' sumn serious like a surgery. I can line that up for you."

Shine looked up slowly, swallowing hard.

Mo continued. "Gimme a day ta see wha' I can do – reasonably – without fucking ya ova as ya, in so many words, said yourself."

Shine nodded, tears swelling again, but he didn't bother hiding them this time. Mo wasn't judging. He understood.

After the brief talk with Big Mo, Shine felt it was best to go be by Angela's side, and Big Mo didn't hesitate to offer him a ride. Thirty minutes later, they were in Mo's SUV, riding in quiet understanding, as Shine stared out the window, bracing himself to see his sleeping angel once he reached the hospital.

The cold air outside hit him instantaneously, but it didn't do a damn thing to numb the pain grinding in his chest. By the time he reached the hospital parking lot, his hands were shaking – not from fear but from the weight of everything he was carrying.

Inside, the luminous hospital lights again felt too bright. All the hospital's interior seemed too clean compared to the chaos in his head. He stepped up to the front desk where the night nurse looked up with tired eyes.

"Visiting Angela Mathis," he said, keeping his voice low.

The nurse recognized him from the night before and nodded gently. "Room 214. You can go on in."

He thanked her under his breath and walked down the hallway, each step feeling heavier than the last. When he pushed open the door, the steady beep of the monitors greeted him – cold, steady reminders she was alive… but barely hanging on.

Angela lay there still as porcelain: tubes, wires, then the machines breathing for her. The sight broke something in him every time he saw it.

Shine pulled a chair up close and sat down slowly, placing elbows on his knees, hands clasped. For a long moment, he just stared at her face; it was a little pale and unusually quiet. She had always been the loud one. The bright one. The talk-too-much, laugh-too-hard little sister who annoyed him and loved him in the same breath.

"An... Ang..." he whispered, voice trembling. "Damn, ya look so small now."

His eyes burned, but he didn't blink. He let the memories wash through him – her running up behind him yelling "Shiiine!" whenever she wanted something, her stealing his snacks and his hoodies. Her crying into his chest the day she didn't make the cheer team. Her laughing when he tried to teach her how to rap, and she kept rhyming "cat" with "cat."

He swallowed hard, leaning in closer.

"You 'member when you were younger, and ya swore you saw a ghost in da closet?" he said softly. "I ain't sleep fo' four nights cause you kept crawlin' in my bed like, 'Shine, scoot ova!'"

A tiny smile cracked through his pain before it faded.

"Ya always been brave, Ang. Braver than me."

He reached out and took her hand – small, cold, weak. He squeezed it like he could somehow push life back into her.

"Listen... I don' know if ya can hear me. I hope you can. But today..." He paused, breathing unevenly. "T'day gon' be da first time I ever robbed somebody."

His jaw tightened, but he kept going.

"I know, I know... it sound crazy. But I swear ta God, you ain' got ta worry bout me getting hurt. I'm gon' ta be careful. Real careful. Cause ain' doing this for no street shit. I do it for you."

A tear slid down his cheek and dropped onto her bedsheet.

"I gon' ta get this money, Ang. All of it. Whateva dem doctas want, whateva they need – I gon' get it. And you going to wake up. You gon' wake up and be mad wid me fa actin' like I some kind superhero." He chuckled weakly. "An' I'ma tell you da truth... I ain' no hero. Just your big brotha who loves you mo' than life, girly."

He leaned back in the chair, wiping his face with shaky hands.

Minutes turned into hours. He sat there quietly, watching her chest rise and fall with the machine's rhythm. Listening to the beeps. Thinking. Praying in ways he didn't even know how to pray.

He checked the time on his phone.

Only an hour and a half left before he had to meet T-Man and Blow for the lick.

His stomach twisted, fear mixing with determination. He looked at Angela one more time – really looked at her. Then he stood, brushing his hand across her hair gently.

"I'll be back, Ang," he whispered. "Next time… I gon' have da money."

He took one last breath of the room – the hospital smell, the humming machines, the fragile hope holding everything together – and walked out.

Each step away from her felt like walking deeper into the unknown.

CHAPTER SEVEN

Pulling the black Nike hoodie over his head, Shine stared at his reflection for a long minute. His eyes were still swollen from the hospital visit with Angela. Everything inside him felt paper-thin, his resolve crumbling a little more every second she stayed trapped in that silent, helpless sleep. Too many times he'd already prayed – prayed she wasn't suffering, prayed she wasn't aware of anything, prayed it was just some peaceful dream she was floating in.

His jaw clenched. His eyes glazed over again, and he forced himself to rub the tears away before they had the chance to fall. He needed his mind focused if he was really about to take this money. His nerves were jittery, but he knew enough – from the movies, from the stories, from the streets he grew up in, to know that going into his first lick trembling was how people got killed. Blow and T-Man were his brothers. He wasn't about to put them in danger because he couldn't control his emotions.

He stepped out of his room and walked toward his mother's bedroom door. He pressed his ear against it and listened a second, hoping maybe she was asleep… or maybe awake enough to look like herself again. He cracked the door open. His mother lay curled in the covers, the same way she had every moment she wasn't at the hospital or working herself numb. Seeing her like this stabbed at something raw in him. The light of both their worlds was dimming fast.

He walked in quietly, unsure if she was awake.

"Ma," he whispered, kneeling beside her. "I'm 'bout ta step out, clear my head a lil bit. I love you."

She didn't respond, but he leaned down and kissed the top of her head anyway, gently, like he used to when he was younger after she'd fallen asleep on the couch after long shifts.

He backed out, closed the door softly, then locked the front door behind him. Pulling the hoodie fully over his head, he saw T-Man's car waiting at the curb, the engine running. The mission was set in motion.

T-Man was behind the wheel. Blow sat next to him, scrolling through his phone, a slight grin playing on his lips.

"Wha' good?" Shine said, sliding into the backseat.

"Wassup, my boi?" Blow said, twisting around. "Ya ready?"

"It either now or neva," Shine replied.

"Most definitely." Blow reached down between his legs and pulled up two options. "Look ya, I know you a virgin ta dis kinda shit, so pick whateva ya think ya gon' be comfortable wit'. *Slugger Johnson*," he held up the Charles Daly Hunch short-barrel shotgun, "or Black Baby," he said, tapping the Glock 9 against the shotgun.

Shine didn't even need a full second. He'd never fired a shotgun before. His nerves were already shaking under his skin. Messing with that kind of kickback tonight was a fast way to end up placing somebody on a T-shirt.

"The pistol," he said.

Blow lifted the Glock for him to take. Shine wrapped his fingers around the grip. The metal felt cold, heavy – and it was black as the night.

For a moment, he just stared at it… then Angela's face flashed across his mind. Her small hand in his. The beeping of the machines. The fear in his mother's eyes.

He was about to turn himself into a person he had never been.

All because of his love for her.

The ride took a long thirty minutes. And for Shine, most of it was spent in heavy silence. The city rolled by outside the windows in a blur of streetlights and shadows, but Shine barely registered any of it. His knee bounced the whole time, and every few minutes, he tightened his grip on the Glock like it might steady the shaking inside him.

"We a block away from the target's house," Blow finally spoke, then he went over the plan again. Shine listened, replaying everything Blow had explained earlier. His part was simple: follow Blow's lead and secure whoever Blow wasn't already on. T-Man would handle the rest.

Shine nodded slowly, taking a deep breath as the car eased closer to the neighborhood. His pulse quickened. His throat became even tighter.

He noticed T-Man hadn't said a single word the whole ride. He sat stiff behind the wheel, eyes forward, jaw locked in place. It was like he was there without being there. Shine didn't know where his head was at, but he wasn't about to ask. Not tonight.

Blow's phone lit up, breaking the tension. He glanced down at the screen.

"It Draco and one mo' nigga in dere. He in da bedroom, and da other nigga stretched on the couch," Blow said. "So, we stick ta da plan. In an' out. Easy peasy."

Shine swallowed hard and closed his eyes for a moment. He took another deep breath, trying to calm the wild drums pounding in his chest. Angela's face filled his mind again – small, peaceful, and slowly fading. The machines. The silence. The fear. Everything he stood to lose if this didn't go right.

Losing her was not an option.

After a few more minutes of slow rolling through the neighborhood, T-Man finally pulled the car over. Blow leaned forward, scanning the dimly lit street.

"House right roun' da block," he said. "Once I get da text – it on." Then, he twisted in his seat to look Shine dead in his eyes. "My nigga… no mattah how many of these we got ta pull, we gon' get dat money fa lil Ange. I promise ya that."

He turned back to the window and sat like he'd done this a million and one times.

T-Man finally broke his silence, his voice low and cold. "Or we gon' force dem people ta do it."

Shine stared at the back of the headrest where T-Man's head was parked, then looked out his own window at the quiet street outside. A wave of gratitude washed through him. Whatever happened tonight, at least he wasn't facing it alone. He had brothers beside him.

And for Angela, that meant everything.

CHAPTER EIGHT

Chelsea stood in the bathroom with the door locked, her thumbs trembling as she sent the text. As soon as it delivered, she slipped the phone into her back pocket and stared up at her reflection.

The mirror didn't do her any favors tonight. It showed everything she tried to hide – the shine on her cheek where she'd been sweating, the twitch in her bottom lip, the way her pupils shook with fear. She pressed both palms on the edge of the sink and whispered a shaky prayer.

"God… don' let dis be da nigh' I die behind somebody else's mess."

She closed her eyes and felt her chest tighten. The compromising situations Blow kept throwing her into were starting to stack too high. A few times before, it hadn't bothered her. The men she'd set up were nobodies – outskirt dudes, small timers who nobody would miss except maybe their plug. But this time?

Draco?

Her stomach rolled. Draco wasn't some random corner boy; he was a stamped mark in Charleston. His name held weight in every inner neighborhood from the Eastside to North Central. A man who moved silent and violently, who didn't smile unless something bad was happening to somebody else. Even his silence felt like a threat.

Chelsea remembered the first time she saw him – how he rolled through with that deadpan stare, the type that made grown men shrink. He wasn't a reckless loudmouth. He was the kind of dangerous that didn't need to say much. And she chose to line all this up tonight, for Blow.

The dude she had too much love for, more than she ever admitted. Someone she let get into her head, then her heart, and now into the places her common sense used to live. She hated that he had that hold. She hated the fact even more that she couldn't seem to break it.

"If dis shit don' make me stop, it ah be because I ain't round to do it," she whispered to her reflection.

She stared at herself one more time, adjusting her hair, wiping her bottom lip. She checked that her conscience was exactly where she left it – untouched in her mental closet. Everything had to look natural.

With a deep breath, she flushed the toilet, just for the sound, washed her hands, and stepped out.

Draco was in the back bedroom, sitting at the edge of the bed in nothing but boxers, with his legs spread wide, watching her with that smug smirk that made her skin crawl. His gold chain lay heavy across his tattooed chest.

"So, I got ta wait all week on your promise?" he asked, his voice deep and slow like he had all the time in the world.

Chelsea gave him a seductive smirk. "I say a lotta shit. So please… do remind me."

She kept the role alive even as her eyes darted to her purse – still exactly where she left it. Good.

Chelsea stepped out of her designer heels and sank down on her knees between his legs, sliding a hand inside his boxer's slit. He let out a grunt.

She kissed him – soft, slow, calculated – then trailed down his neck and continued on lower, circling her tongue around his nipple. Draco's head fell back, a heavy breath leaving him. He relaxed.

She freed his manhood with both hands, warming her palms with spit. Her hands moved with practiced ease, but her eyes kept flicking upward, pretending she was searching for some emotion in him – a connection she knew damn well didn't exist. It was all part of the act.

A bead of saliva gathered on her tongue. She let it fall onto his tip, which caused his body to slightly twitch. Then, she paused, meeting his eyes.

"You remembuh' the rules?" she asked softly. It wasn't really a question – more like a warning.

Draco smirked, drunk off a quarter pint of Hennessy. "Remine Daddy."

Chelsea breathed in through her nose and lowered her head.

She moved with a slow, steady rhythm, her focus locked on him, trying to pull Draco deeper into her spell. His breathing shifted – rougher, heavier. His muscles tightened, and his hand slid into her hair, gripping her with growing intensity.

And even though she told him – not to burst in her mouth – Draco did what Draco always wanted to do.

He grabbed the back of her head and groaned, releasing himself into her throat.

Chelsea jerked back too late, choking on the taste, before spitting it out toward his abdomen.

"Nigga!" she snapped, wiping her tongue with her palm, disgusted.

Draco laughed – a deep, mocking, drunk laugh. "Mami, stop playin'. Ya knew how Daddy get down."

Chelsea shot him a dirty look and stormed off back into the bathroom, slamming the door behind her. She turned on the faucet, rinsed out her mouth hard, rubbing her tongue against her teeth.

But the rage wasn't real. The disgust wasn't new. It was all part of the show.

She grabbed her hidden phone and sent the quick text: "Now."

Her heart pounded as she dropped the phone back into her pocket. She wiped her mouth, checked herself one last time, and stepped out.

She snatched up her things and shoved her feet into her heels. Draco followed her out of the bedroom, still chuckling as he tugged his boxers up.

"Come on, gal. Ya know you like'um…"

She didn't let him finish. She headed straight for the front door.

Draco's boy, Tune, was laid back on the couch, playing the game, eyes halfway on her as she breezed by.

Before either man could really process it, she unlocked both locks, yanked open the door, then the burglar bar.

"Chelsea! Hol' up…" Draco called from behind her, now realizing something was off.

He reached her just as she stepped out…

And then the world exploded. Three masked men rushed the porch at full speed.

Chelsea screamed – loud and terrified, the acting was Oscar-worthy. Draco stumbled backward.

Everything happened a little too fast.

Draco spun around, confusion cutting across his face – too drunk, too slow.

Blow hit the porch first, shotgun raised, the barrel damn near kissing Draco's nose.

"Don' move, nigga," Blow snarled, his voice vibrating with murderous focus.

Draco froze for half a heartbeat – just long enough for Blow to shove the shotgun forward, ramming him back through the doorway. Draco stumbled, lost his footing, and crashed onto the hardwood with a grunt.

Inside, the stale smell of Hennessy and blunt smoke hung thick. The TV flashed bright colors across the living room.

The other dude was laid back on the couch. Confused and shocked, he blinked dumbly at the intruders. His reaction time was as slow as syrup. His assault rifle leaned against the couch arm, untouched. The pistol tucked in his waistband might as well have been a brick.

T-Man came in silent and deadly.

One second, the drunk dude was sitting there. The next, T-Man was on him, pressing the muzzle of his Glock against the man's temple so hard it left an indent.

"Try it," T-Man whispered, cold as a morgue drawer.

Draco, still on the floor, pushed up on one elbow, dazed and struggling to focus. "Wha' —wha' da fuck y'all think ya doin'?" he slurred. "Do ya know who da fuck I is?"

Blow chambered a new round, the click-clack echoing like a threat, so Draco could really understand how much they cared.

He stepped over Draco, towering above him. "Duh, nigga. Ya da reason we heah." Blow bent down, voice tightening. "Now where da fu—"

Before he could finish, Chelsea screamed behind them.

"Wha the fuck you doing?! I'm no'…"

Blow spun around sharply. And what he saw made his blood pressure spike. Shine had Chelsea by the neck, dragging her backward into the house, pistol pressed to the side of her head. She clawed at his wrist, choking, eyes wide and shocked as hell.

For a split second, Blow's mask of control cracked.

"Shine… the hell ya…" He caught himself mid-sentence, but the name was out. It was too late.

T-Man's glare shot across the room – sharp and knowing. Blow felt the mistake cut through the air like a blade.

They had rules. This broke one.

Blow exhaled sharply, recalibrating, hiding panic under grit. He squared his shoulders, pointing the shotgun toward the door.

"Push ha out an' shut da door."

Shine froze for a moment.

Chelsea's eyes darted between them, confused, terrified, then something else clicked in Shine's mind. It hit him like a cold slap. She was the inside person. She was the one who'd been texting.

That was why Blow wanted her gone.

Shine's jaw tightened. Forcefully, he shoved her outside, never breaking aim. Chelsea stumbled across the porch, gasping for breath, stumbling down the steps in her heels. Shine slammed the door behind her.

The house instantly shrank into a box of danger and stale, suffocating mentalities.

"Zip 'em," Blow ordered.

Shine and T-Man got to work. T-Man yanked the dude off the cushions face first, zip-tying his wrists until the plastic dug into his skin. The drunk man whimpered, half confused, half sobered by fear.

Shine tied Draco, who struggled more out of ego than strength. His wrists shook as Shine cinched the ties tight.

"Wha' da fuck is dis, man?!" Draco barked.

Blow stepped close. His breath was hot with fury. "Since you so hard-headed, T… show 'um."

T-Man grinned a hungry little smirk.

Moving from the couch, he grabbed Draco by the hair and drove his fist into Draco's face. Blood splattered across the floorboards.

Draco choked, coughing thick red onto his chest.

T-Man hit him again.

And again – and again.

Draco's face swelled instantly. One eye closed. Teeth clinked as blood pooled around his tongue.

Finally, he threw his head back, gasping. "'Ight-'ight!"

T-Man paused mid-swing, knuckles dripping.

Draco spat a glob of red and laughed – dark and ugly. "'Ight… I give y'all dat shit," he said, smirking through the blood. "But you Gullah niggas… don' even know wha' da fuck you startin'."

His words dripped with venom. His smile curled into something mocking. He wasn't scared.

Blow leaned in, pressing the shotgun to Draco's swollen cheek.

"Well," Blow said, voice low and dangerous, "you 'bout ta show us."

The room fell silent except for Draco's bleeding breath, the faint hum of the video game still running, and the pounding hearts of three men now fully committed to doing what was necessary.

CHAPTER NINE

The backseat felt too small for all the noise in his head. Shine sat hunched over, the Glock warm and heavy in his lap, even though he hadn't touched it since leaving that house. The leather smelled like sweat and gun oil, and every time the car hit a pothole, his jaw clenched on instinct. Outside, the city rolled by in slow-motion, streetlights dragging like theater spotlights over scenes he couldn't un-see.

He kept replaying Blow's voice – how it sounded when it slipped saying his name. How easy a name could turn a robbery into two murders. The way Blow said *"Shine"* had hung in the air like a bell toll.

And then everything after that happened so fast. The panic. The sudden shift in their faces. The look T-Man gave when he realized what had to be done.

Then the two hard sounds – hard and final – that filled the house with a silence that wasn't silence at all.

There was a memory Shine couldn't shake. The way Draco crum-pled. And the way the other man – the one on the couch – was gone before Draco even ceased to exist.

Shine's stomach turned every time he tried to breathe. He'd come out of that house with money – thirty-six grand and the weight of a few bags of weed – yet the money felt like someone else's sin pressed into his palm. It warmed his fingers and chilled his gut at the same time. He'd thought tonight would be a clean line between desperate and saving, get the cash, hand it over to the hospital, watch Angela wake up. Instead, he was knotted up in two dead men.

They'd given him the money without an argument. Blow shoved the stacks into his hands like an apology, and T-Man nodded like brothers do – no speeches, just the work of moving fast, protecting the bloodline.

"Weh' got you," Blow had said. "If ya down for more, I got setups. If not – we still gon' ta feed you. We got lil Ange." They meant it. Hearing that softened something inside of Shine. They were reckless and rough and wrong in ways that would haunt him later, but they'd chosen his family when they could have chosen themselves.

That was the part that made his chest ache the worst: love and violence braided together until he couldn't tell which was which. He respected them – maybe more than he ever wanted to – and hated them for the cost they were bound to bear. He hated himself for letting the hate for the hospital bills push him into a dark corner where killing was an option. He'd never imagined being the kind of person, whose hands touched blood that night.

Shine's mind ran like a busted engine, firing off every scenario at once, tossing together pieces of a future he hadn't planned for. If this was the price of saving Angela, could he really live with it? Could he carry the weight of more risk, more blood, more nights that didn't end? And if he refused Blow's other setups, would they still risk their lives for him, or would he be left with only scraps of money – and the bodies – to haunt him, alone, exposed, and hunted by everyone with a reason to?

Practical thoughts slotted into the panic like old habits. He started running through the numbers, trying to find the math that would fix everything: three hundred and twenty thousand – split, laundered, moved. How many licks would it take? How many days of planning; how many routes — how many victims?

He pictured the kinds of hits he'd only seen in movies and heard during moments of corner talk – the jewelry drop in the trunk, the courier with the cash bag, the take from a stash house. Each idea came with its own risks, a list of everything that could go wrong: a silent alarm, a witness, a wrong move, the siren wail that ended everything.

His brain cataloged the worst-case scenarios like a man drafting a will – what to do if they chased him, who to call if he disappeared, how to cover his tracks without losing his soul.

But even the schemes sounded small beneath the weight of what he had now.

Money solved bills, not ghosts. Money bought time, maybe surgery, maybe a shot at her waking up, but it didn't buy forgiveness.

He thought about Angela's face – the pale cheeks under the slick hospital light, the small sounds the machines made – and the image cut deeper than any worry about being caught. He promised himself, again and again in the cramped backseat, that whatever happened next would be for her, exactly like this had been – for her laugh, for the hoodie she stole, for the way she used to snore like a little motor. That promise felt like a tether and like shackles all at once.

Shine pictured his mother's face – the hollow look from the couch, the way she folded into herself whenever she wasn't at work or at the hospital. If he walked away from this money now, what would be the result? If he leaned into Blow's offers, would he wake up in some fast car with sirens in the rearview? The answers were jagged, the edges cutting his sleep before he had a chance.

T-Man tossed him a cigarette; Shine shook his head because his hands were too jittery to hold the thing steady. Blow reached back and gave his shoulder a quick, brotherly shake. He smiled yet said nothing. Words at this point felt useless anyway.

He let the city hum around him and tried to sort the crowd of thoughts into something like a plan, though every plan had a movie ending, and every movie ending felt like someone else's life.

He thought about running, about changing his name, about cashing out and disappearing somewhere the hospital bills couldn't find him. Waking Angela from her slumber and taking her with him. He imag-ined piling the money into a duffel, getting on a bus, starting fresh.

But under the fear sat the stubborn, ugly truth: he had no passport, no safety net, no skills that paid without blood. No Angela. Only two men who'd killed for him and the same hands that had touched murder.

The car rolled quieter, and the city's neon bled into the windows. Blow steered like a man who did things and regretted them in private. T-Man stared forward like he was already three moves ahead, an unread ledger in his eyes. Shine folded himself smaller in the seat, listening to the thump of his pulse like a metronome counting down for whatever came next.

When they dropped him off, it was almost ten. The house looked small under the streetlamp, a box of familiar shadows. His hands trembled when he fumbled with the key – simple, habitual, the motion of coming home – but right now, it all felt foreign.

He stepped inside, and the floorboard complained in a way that made him wince. The air smelled like old dinner and his mother's perfume, like a life that had been paused and left on the table.

He silently closed the door behind him slowly, listening for anything.

Shine listened and stepped inside the dim kitchen. The lights above the stove hummed softly, shining just enough to reveal his mother and Uncle Jeff sitting at the table, their faces heavy, shadows under their eyes. But it was his mother's face that hit him the hardest – her cheeks wet, her fingers trembling around a balled-up napkin.

She looked up, voice cracking.

"Where you been, Shine?" Her eyes flicked to the clock then back to him – scared, exhausted, desperate.

Shine didn't bother to lie. His chest felt bruised from everything happening. "I went an' got some of da money fo' Angela."

He swung the small tote bag off his shoulder, unzipped it, and poured the few stacks of cash onto the table. The sound of it – soft thuds of rubber-banded money – felt unreal in the quiet kitchen.

His mother's breath caught. "Shine…" She rose halfway from her chair, staring at the money as if it were radioactive. "Where ya get this from?"

He ignored the question. "It thirty-six thousand. I working on da res'."

Her hand flew to her chest, and she shook her head so hard her braids swung.

"Shine, no. No, baby, this-this ain't yo' place!" Her voice cracked into raw pain. "I'm yo' mama. I s'posed ta handle this. Not you out heah… doin' God knows wha' fo' money!"

She started crying harder, wiping at her face like she was trying to erase the moment. "I'll figur' it out, Shine. I calling the insurance people again tomorra…"

Shine snapped, every emotion he'd been drowning in finally boiling over. "Dey ain' gonna do shit!" The words ripped out of him. "They not gon' save Angela. She's…" He swallowed, chest tight. "She's gon' die, Ma!"

The room felt like it tilted. Then…

SMACK.

His mother's palm met his cheek so fast he didn't even see her move.

Silence immediately swallowed the kitchen.

She gasped at her own hand then covered her mouth as tears streamed harder. "Don'-don' ya eva speak death ova my baby." Her voice shook violently. "No, not in me house. Not 'bout Angela."

Shine blinked, jaw tight, throat burning.

His mother turned away, shoulders trembling, and stumbled toward her bedroom.

"I cain't…" she choked. "I cain't heah that. I cain't…"

She disappeared down the hallway, one hand cupped over her face, as she sobbed into it.

The silence she left behind felt heavy enough to crush him.

His uncle, Jeff, stood slowly. He put a firm hand on Shine's shoulder, grounding him. "Come take a ride with me, nephew."

They drove in silence for several minutes, the city drifting past in a blur of streetlights. Finally, Uncle Jeff exhaled long and low, like there were words he'd been holding back for years.

"I rememba' when you and Angela were born," he began, voice

softer than usual. "Ya mama, your daddy… man, we were so damn happy. Y'all came into this world an' lit it up." He chuckled sadly, eyes never leaving the road. "Angela was so small. Lawd, she was so tiny. Looked like she ain even weigh a bag of suga. But she was beautiful. Bright-eyed from the jump."

Shine stared out his window, jaw tight. Hearing her name hurt.

Uncle Jeff continued, hands flexing on the wheel. "All I eva wanted was the best fo' you two."

Another pause.

His voice dropped lower. "Ya ain' wrong fo' doing wha' you had to do."

Shine looked at him, genuinely surprised. All his life, Uncle Jeff had been the most upstanding person he knew – someone whose name was never whispered in scandal or suspicion. Never once had Shine caught him in wrongdoing, never once had he imagined his uncle bending rules for himself. So hearing him saying this – it made Shine pause. It made him think, really think, about the lines people crossed when it mattered and what it meant to fight for something worth the risk.

Uncle Jeff nodded. "Ain' a damn thing wrong with a man fightin' fo' his blood. But you got ta be careful. This life? It take more than it a give back."

He sighed again.

"Your mama… she got too much faith in this crooked-ass system. Think paperwork and phone calls going save ya sister. But nothin' legit is gon' ta cover them surgery fees. Nothin'."

Shine stared at him. Again – he had never heard Uncle Jeff talk like this.

That was when Uncle Jeff turned into a parking lot Shine didn't recognize. He cut the engine, leaving them in the thick quiet.

For a long moment, they just sat there. Uncle Jeff kept his eyes forward.

"Ten years, Shine," he softly began. "Ten years I been watchin' the ins and outs of my job. Seein' how things move. Countin' otha people's blessings and wonderin'… wonderin' if I had the heart ta take what was needed."

He shook his head.

"But back then? I didn't have ah reason big enough ta take the risk."

He finally turned, looking Shine directly in the eyes. "Ya acted out of love. Ya did everythin' ya thought ya needed ta do. But that still ain' enough."

Shine swallowed hard.

Uncle Jeff nodded toward the dark building in front of them.

"But I know what will be."

CHAPTER TEN

Sleep didn't come easily to Shine that night. It punished him.

In the dream, he was right back in Draco's house. The air was thick with smoke and fear, the same ugly mix from the night before. Draco's body hit the floor again, that dull, heavy thud echoing in his skull like someone slamming a car door inside his mind.

Shine watched the blood soak in the fine fabric of the carpet like it had the perfect place to settle. The other dude – the one whose name he'd never get to know – kept blinking at him with that wide, confused stare, like he couldn't understand why life chose this moment to let go of him.

Then, the dream shifted. Now, Shine was outside, standing in the middle of King Street as a long, city transit bus rumbled in front of him. He didn't know how he got there – only that Angela was inside. She sat in the window, palms pressed hard against the glass, tears streaming, face lit up in flashing red as the brake lights pulsed.

"SHINE!" she screamed.

He bolted toward the bus, slapping the metal side, trying to find the front door. But every time he lunged, it slid farther out of reach, rolling forward like the road was swallowing it. Angela banged on the glass harder, her voice cracking, her little fingers leaving smudges he couldn't wipe away.

"STOP! PLEASE! ANGELA!"

His throat burned. His legs felt like concrete blocks, but he kept running – reaching – failing. The driver never looked at him. The bus picked up speed. Angela's scream twisted into something smaller, something fading.

Shine pushed harder, chest collapsing in on itself.

"ANGELA!" His voice bounced around the street, echoing until…

A hand shook him.

Then another, harder this time.

"Shine! Shine! Baby! Wake up!"

He shot up in bed, drenched in sweat, chest swelling. His mother stood over him with fear stamped all over her face. Shine looked around the room like he didn't know where he was.

"You was screaming ha name," she cried, wiping his forehead. "Baby, ya was hollering like somebody wa'…"

Shine swallowed hard, trying to catch his breath. "I good," he muttered, sliding away from her touch.

"Shine…" she whispered.

He couldn't look at her. He didn't want her to see what was eating him alive – the guilt, the fear, the images from the night before. He turned toward the wall, rubbing his forehead.

"I said I good."

Her face broke even more as she covered her mouth with her tears spilling from her eyes. Without another word, she turned and left his room, the soft click of the door sounding like disappointment.

It took him almost twenty minutes before he could breathe normal again.

He washed his face, pulled on a jacket, and stepped outside just as T-Man walked up the sidewalk. T-Man dapped him but paused, studying his face.

"Ya good?" T-Man asked.

Shine hesitated – a bit too long – then nodded. "Yeah." It was a lie, thin and see-through. "Come 'ere," he said, glancing around. "Let get in da car real quick."

They slid into T-Man's Crown Vic. Shine looked out each window again, paranoid, replaying the murders, the blood, the nightmare. Finally, he asked, "Ya talked to Blow?"

"Nuh," T-Man said. "Da boi s'posed ta be dumping dem bags dis mornin'. Why?"

Shine scratched his jaw, breath heavy. "Look ya, I got a lick set up… got da ins an' outs down ta da tee…"

T-Man cut in, eyebrows raised. "Who da boi?"

Shine shook his head slowly. "Not who," he said. "but what."

T-Man looked at him sideways. Shine almost regretted bringing it up; this was his bro, but T-Man and Blow had robbed before, small-time hustlers, but never the kind of thing Shine's uncle had placed in his mind. Nothing close.

But he'd already opened the door.

Minutes later, the two of them were pulled up outside Blow's cousin's place. Blow hopped in the backseat, smelling like Hennessy and cheap smoke.

"Where weh gon'?" Blow asked.

Shine gestured out the window. "Downtown."

As they rolled toward King Street, they saw workers roping off areas, setting up tents and vendor booths for the "2nd Sunday on King" event. Blow squinted at the crowd forming, confused.

"Aye, why we down heah?" Blow asked. "Wha' ya got gon'?"

Shine exhaled, staring straight ahead. "Las' night… my uncle been explainin' some shit ta me 'bout risk. 'Bout why folks stay broke. He say if ya keep hittin' small time, ya gon' always be pullin' juggs fa lil to no money. He say da risk go up every time, but the payout don't. An' eventually, ya either dead or get caught wit' nuthin ta show fo' it."

Blow raised an eyebrow. "Boi, wha' kinda sermon is dis? Get ta da point."

Shine nodded at T-Man. "Pull in dat lot."

T-Man parked in the same spot he'd been with his uncle the night before. Shine stared at a building across the lot. The morning sun glinted off the glass doors.

"It," Shine said quietly, "is somethin' dat gon' pay fo' Angela's surgery – an' leave money in all our pockets."

Blow and T-Man looked at him, confused but listening.

"Wha' ya talking about, gangsta?" T-Man asked.

Blow cut his eyes toward the building, already piecing it together.

He smirked. "Ah bank."

T-Man blinked hard. "Bou… wha'?"

Blow leaned forward between the seats. "Dat's exactly wha' he talkin' 'bout." Blow nodded his head in its direction.

Shine nodded once. "Dead ass serious, sho'."

CHAPTER ELEVEN

Shine did everything his uncle told him, step for step, like a man following a map out of hell.

First came the disguises.

They hit up a contractor supply warehouse on the outskirts of Charleston, snatching up three navy-blue workman jumpsuits, the kind painters wore when they were about to do a job. Shine grabbed three respirator masks, latex gloves, and simple ball caps to cover hair and faces. His uncle emphasized the simplest rule:

"Blend in an' don' stand out."

On the way out, Shine spotted a closet door propped open in the back hallway. Inside were hanging racks of catering uniforms – white shirts, black aprons, bowties, the whole nine. With a quick glance down the hallway, T-Man slipped inside and pulled down enough outfits for the three of them plus a spare. They stuffed them under the jumpsuits.

Then they made their way to the next objective.

T-Man drove them toward James Island, where a row of abandoned houses sat behind a construction zone. In the side alley, a white cargo van was parked, unlocked, left by some careless construction worker who'd clocked out too tired to care. T-Man worked the ignition in under thirty seconds. The engine coughed then growled awake.

"Bless da lazy flam boi." Blow smirked as they pulled off.

At a strip mall, Shine bought a bucket of white paint, the thick industrial kind they used for road curbs. He added two metal toolboxes and a set of toy guns just to complete the list. His uncle said that they didn't need real guns because he didn't need anyone dying. Neither T-Man or Blow liked the idea, and Shine had to admit he didn't either. So, he still bought the toy guns for the sake of the list, but they wouldn't be used for their purpose.

Then they hit an online reseller kiosk and purchased the last thing Shine's uncle insisted on:

A KJB Pocket RF Detector. It was a tiny device but crucial. It could detect trackers in bags, radios, anything the bank might hide.

Shine turned the box over in his hand, thinking, *We really bout ta do dis*. His stomach felt like a balled fist.

———

By nightfall, he had Blow and T-Man with him. The trio headed toward the outside bar and grill his uncle chose. The place sat quiet – maybe five people total, scattered far from the porch area where Uncle Jeff waited.

The man looked older than his fifty-something years – beard graying at the chin, eyes that stayed sharp even when relaxed. He nodded as they approached.

Before Shine could speak, Jeff held up a hand. "No names," he muttered. "Ain' nobody in this. Not legally, not conversationally. Just roles."

He looked Blow and T-Man over like a general measuring soldiers.

"Where the fourth?" he asked bluntly. "Told ya – this needs four bodies, not three."

Shine hesitated, shoulders low. "I got somebody in mind," he said. "Jus' ain' brought it ta him yet."

Jeff studied him, reading him the way only an uncle could. "How ya holdin'?" he asked.

Shine gave the kind of shrug that hid everything and nothing.

Jeff nodded then slid his phone – a touchscreen with a glowing map – onto the table.

"A'right. Let get to it."

He zoomed in on a map of King Street, finger tracing routes like a surgeon marking an incision.

"Ya driver – whoeva that end up bein' – gon' park in the tiny lot beside Starbucks. Right yah."

His finger tapped the spot. "The other three? Y'all come in off Radcliffe, totin ya toolboxes an' ya paint. Jumpsuits on. Masks on. Hats. Gloves. Ya painters an' nuttin' more."

Blow leaned forward, squinting. "Dis at noon?"

Jeff nodded. "11:55. That's the midday swing."

T-Man raised a brow. "Da wha'?"

"The noon vault exchange," Jeff clarified. "That's when they move an' count money – inside shuffle. Biggest movement uh them bags. Security relaxes 'cause it routine."

He shifted the map again. "Soon as y'all walk up, dthe man with the paint break formation. He got ta smack the windshield an' the side window – heavy. Blind 'em up."

Blow blinked. "An' da otha two?"

"The otha two secure the space and pepper spray us."

They both froze. "Wha'?" T-Man stiffened.

Jeff finally met their eyes. "I be there. Inside. Outside. Somewheh close. This is ta protect my nephew an' make sho' nobody follow y'all. An' ta make sure nobody get no clean ID on none of you. Ya spray us, that gon' make the chaos real."

They stared like they couldn't tell if he was a genius or insane.

Jeff continued. "Soon as the one inside the truck scan them bags an' toss 'em out to y'all, ya run back through heah – Radcliffe – cut right 'tween the green house and the plaza." His finger slid through the path. "In this alley, two uh y'all strip off them jumpsuits. Third one loads ya bags into the caterin' carts."

Blow interrupted. "Carts?"

Shine nodded. "I already got two."

Uncle Jeff kept going. "Jumpsuits go in the dumpster. Third man bleachin everythin'. Then, ya three push them food carts straight out into the crowd on King Street. Police gon' already be respondin', but they gon' be on foot. They ain' gon' know who's workers an' who's suspects."

He sat back, confidence showing. "Ya cross Morris Street. Blend in. Everyone distracted. Cops gon' be lookin' fo' fast getaway car." He smirked slightly. "I tell them I saw one heading in the opposite direction."

Blow chuckled under his breath. "So wha' – den weh home free?"

Jeff pointed to the map again. "Once ya reach the Starbucks lot, load yah carts into van. Pull out onto Mary Street. Make ah left. From there? You gon'."

He closed the phone. "No deviation. No panic. No hero moves. Jes' precision. Gon' be a cake walk."

Blow leaned back, arms folded. "Nuthin' a cakewalk til it done."

Jeff stared at him calmly. "Then get it done."

CHAPTER TWELVE

T-Man turned the corner slow, the tires humming a low, steady note as the hospital came into view. MUSC Children's didn't look like a place where bad news lived. The white lights were too brilliant, too clean, too peaceful. But for Shine, every step toward that building felt like wading into cold water he wasn't ready for.

"Drop me heah," he murmured.

T-Man eased the car to the curb. "Ya good, bro?"

Shine nodded, but his voice never caught up to the gesture. He closed the door softly, almost like the sound alone could shatter the fragile thread holding him together. He watched the car pull off then took a breath, straightened his hoodie, and walked through the sliding doors.

The hospital air hit him different – sterile, faintly sweet, humming with quiet machines and a quiet sadness only people who'd sat in waiting rooms understood. He moved through the hallway slow, each step grinding the weight of the day deeper into his chest. Two bodies lost to the streets. His name shouted during the robbery. T-Man and Blow standing over Draco. His uncle telling him no names were needed because names could get people killed.

He never imagined any of this – not for him, not for Angela.

When he pushed into her room, the lights were dim, like the world knew she needed softer things. Angela looked small in that bed… too small. The machine beside her breathed in quiet, careful rhythms, reminding Shine that it wasn't just him; something was working hard just to keep her here.

He pulled the chair close, the metal legs scraping quietly across the tile. He sat, elbows on his knees, hands locked together to keep from shaking. His eyes went straight to her face – brown skin too pale, lips a little chapped, braids messy the way she always wore them because she never stayed still long enough to let their mama finish them.

But now she was still. Too still.

Shine lifted her hand gently, like it was glass. Her fingers felt cold, and that alone nearly crushed his chest. "Ang…" he whispered.

Her eyelids didn't flutter. Her fingers didn't curl around his. She didn't smile with her whole face the way she always did when she saw him walk through a door.

A silence settled around him – thick and unforgiving. And in that silence, everything hit him at once.

Draco's blood. Blow yelling his name. His uncle's strict, dangerous blueprint. The money they needed. The life Angela might not get to finish living.

Shine swallowed hard, the taste of metal in his mouth. He leaned forward until his forehead rested against the back of her hand.

"I sorry," he exhaled – barely a sound, more like a confession meant for God and ghosts.

He took another shaky and uneven breath, the kind that broke in the middle.

"I ain' s'posed ta be mixed in all this…" he said quietly. "But I swear, Ang… I ain' lettin' ya go like dis. Not you. Not my baby sister."

His thumb brushed her knuckles, slow and steady. His eyes burned, and he blinked hard, but the tears slipped through anyway – one falling, landing on her wrist, mixing with the thin hospital light.

"Ya heah me?" he whispered. "I bringin' you back. Whateva I got ta do… how far I got ta go… I bringin' you back."

The words weren't loud, but they were carved out of something raw enough to draw blood. He held her hand tighter, as if squeezing it alone could anchor her to this world.

Minutes passed – could've been ten, could've been a hundred. Shine didn't move. He just sat there, letting the hope, the fear, the guilt, and the love tie themselves together in the middle of his chest.

Finally, he straightened up, wiped his face on his sleeve, and looked at her again. This time, his expression was different – harder, sharper, carved with purpose. Almost like a man stepping into a new skin.

He kissed her forehead. "I be back, lil sis," he murmured. "An' next time… I walk in wit' ya miracle."

Then, he stood, took one last look – let it burn itself into him – and walked out the room slow, each step carrying a new version of himself.

A version willing to risk everything. A version already halfway into the dark.

All for Angela.

CHAPTER THIRTEEN

S hine pulled the navy-blue jumpsuit up over his catering outfit, the zipper rasping like a quiet warning. He stopped halfway, staring at his reflection in the small mirror hanging crooked on the back of his bedroom door.

His face looked different. Harder. Older. A little haunted.

He dragged a slow breath in, squared his shoulders, pulled the zipper all the way up, and whispered to himself.

"Ya got dis." Not because he believed it… but because he had to.

He flicked off the light, stepped out the room, and headed for T-Man waiting outside.

They rolled through the neighborhood toward the meet spot, the morning sun just kissing the tops of the buildings. The streets were busy with early workers, joggers, and vendors setting up, but inside the car, there was nothing but the quiet hum of the engine and Shine's heartbeat pounding steady in his ears.

When they reached the lot behind the old laundromat, Blow and Roscoe were already there, leaning on the van. Roscoe flicked his cigarette and smirked at Shine.

"Look ya, boi look like he ready ta fix somebody's cable," Roscoe joked.

Shine couldn't help a half-smile. "Sumn' like dat."

They loaded the carts, the toolboxes, the paint bucket, and the two handguns Blow kept loaded. Blow slid behind the wheel and looked back at them.

"'Ight. Errybody know da play," Blow said. "Roscoe, make sho' da paint hit dem windows hard. Shine, man... spray the shit outta ya uncle."

They all laughed – even Shine – because the tension needed somewhere to go.

Traffic slowed them a little as they headed toward King Street, but the closer they got, the quieter the van became. Blow's jaw was tight. T-Man was bouncing his knee. Roscoe was peeling back the label on the paint bucket.

Shine just stared at his hands. Every time he blinked, he saw Angela.

Beep... Beep... Beep... Her lifeline machine.

He clenched his fists.

Blow parked the van in the lot beside the Starbucks like they'd planned. The smell of roasted coffee drifted through the air as they climbed out. After placing a handgun in each toolbox, Shine and T-Man grabbed the carts. Roscoe carried the paint. They adjusted their respirator masks to sit under their chins, not over their faces – no reason to draw eyes yet.

King Street was alive. Folding tables lined the sidewalks, vendors hammering decorations for the "2nd Sunday on King" event. Music played faintly from a portable speaker nearby. The crowd was thick enough to hide inside of – just like Shine's uncle said.

They pushed forward, moving in rhythm, heads low.

After a minute, Shine noticed three police moving through the crowd – talking to vendors, peeking around corners. His pulse jumped.

Their pace slowed just a little bit.

T-Man muttered, "Damn..."

But the officers never even looked their way. They walked right by them, too busy arguing with a street vendor about blocking a fire lane.

They kept going. Shine guided them toward the alley beside Radcliffe. Once they reached it, they parked the carts in the shadows and started prepping.

Toolboxes out. Respirator masks up. Latex gloves snapped into place.

The bucket of paint opened; Roscoe lifted the top just enough for that strong chemical scent to drift.

Shine checked his watch. 11:49.

"Six minutes out," he whispered.

He peeked over Radcliffe. Through the few moving bodies and cars, he spotted the GardaWorld armored truck rolling up to the curb beside the Wells Fargo.

His pulse hit the gas pedal inside him.

"Heah we go," Roscoe said under his breath, lifting the paint bucket lid farther. Their legs worked in rhythm as they closed the distance.

11:51. Two guards stepped out the truck.

T-Man frowned. "Ah thought yo' uncle say it was gon' be him an' one mo' security guy?"

Shine's eyes never left the guards. "Does it mattah?"

It didn't. Not to him. Not anymore.

Roscoe moved first, breaking off toward the left as they crossed Radcliffe Road. Nobody paid them attention; everyone was too busy with the event.

The bank doors opened. Shine spotted his uncle walking out carrying a small clipboard, playing his role perfectly.

They approached each other at the same time. The guards greeted each other, nodding and laughing over something on the clipboard.

Shine and T-Man pulled their weapons in unison…

And then – *SPLOOSH!*

Paint exploded across the windshield and the driver's side window of the truck, thick white smearing the glass like a sudden snowstorm. Everyone flinched. The guards turned – too late.

"GET DA FUCK ON DA GROUND!" T-Man barked, shoving one with the muzzle.

The guards reached for their guns, but when they saw two respirator-masked men charging and another splashing paint by the madman, they froze. They dropped.

"Stretch out ya arms! Palms FLAT!" T-Man ordered.

Shine moved fast – pepper spray out, unleashing two hard bursts into the guards' faces. They screamed and coughed, twisting on the ground.

His uncle tried not to react, but Shine saw it. He sprayed him too.

Sorry, Unc… Shine thought. *Ain' no favorites out heah.*

Roscoe was already inside the back of the truck, scanning bag after bag. They heard the thuds – one, two, three, four – hitting the pavement like bricks wrapped in canvas.

"Got two mo' – weh might well!" Roscoe yelled.

Shine scooped one, and T-Man grabbed two. Roscoe carried three and jumped out the truck, damn near falling to the pavement

They sprinted back across Radcliffe. Shine kept glancing over his shoulder. His breaths were sharp, cutting into his lungs.

His heart hammered like it wanted out.

People were noticing something was wrong now. Heads turned. However, no one shouted for police.

Shine and his crew were diving back into the alley. They reached the carts and immediately peeled off the blue jumpsuits. The air felt colder on their skin.

Roscoe threw his jumpsuit into the dumpster; T-Man yanked the bleach jug from his hands.

"Nah, ya too damn loud!" T-Man snapped, splashing bleach across the pile of blue fabric. The chemical smell burst through the alley.

Shine already had his cart rolling. T-Man and Roscoe followed, blending back into the flow of people.

Then, shouting came from some distance behind them. As they merged into the moving crowd, police whistles could be heard. Shine looked right.

Those same three officers were now shoving through the crowd, causing people to stumble aside. One pointed toward the bank.

Shit.

Shine bumped into a man who'd stopped in front of him. The guy turned, confused, mouth halfway open…

Then, an officer plowed into him from behind, sending him stumbling forward with a curse.

Shine's hand dropped to his waistband instinctively. T-Man saw it and slapped his cart into Shine's side.

Shine snapped his eyes toward him. T-Man gave him a sharp nod, as if saying, *Keep goin'.*

The three of them kept pushing the carts, weaving through the thinning crowd, until the Starbucks parking lot finally came into view. Blow was leaning against the van, cigarette burning between two fingers, like he was posing for a poster. As soon as he spotted Shine and T-Man, he straightened up, crushed the cigarette in his palm, and stuffed it into his pocket before anyone could even blink.

"Come on, come yah," he muttered, swinging the van's rear doors open.

They rolled the carts in fast – no wasted motion, no pointless talking, just adrenaline and instinct. Blow hopped into the driver's seat, T-Man slid in beside him, and Shine and Roscoe climbed into the back, breath still jagged, nerves sizzling.

"No one following?" Blow asked, eyes glued to the mirrors.

T-Man shook his head. "Ain' see nobody."

They pulled out, slow at first, then eased into the route Uncle Jeff had laid out like scripture.

Roscoe bounced once in his kneeled position, unable to hold the energy in. "Nigga, weh 'bout ta ball!" he blurted out, damn near vibrating.

T-Man shot him a hard look. "Nigga, we ain' in da clear yet."

Roscoe gave him a side-eye, lips curled. "Aw, man, heah ya go wit' dat jinxing shit."

Before T-Man could respond, Shine snapped, "Nigga, shut da fuck up."

His voice carried a weight even he didn't expect. He kept looking out the back window, then the front, eyes flicking like a man waiting for a ghost to show itself. His fingers tapped his knee, leg bouncing. His heart had been racing since the second he ran from the bank, and deep down, Shine knew it wasn't going to slow until every dime was in Big Mo's hands.

He kept replaying everything in his head, the paint splash, the guards' hands going up, the screams behind the respirator mask, his uncle on the ground wiping his eyes from the spray. The adrenaline was still streaking through him like electricity.

The van rolled smooth for about ten minutes. It was the kind of smooth that made paranoia whisper louder.

They turned onto a side street, passing a row of old Charleston houses, when Blow's eyes caught something in the mirror.

And just like that, he slammed the brakes.

T-Man jerked forward, hand bracing against the glove box. "Wha' up?" he barked, looking out both windows like threats could materialize out of thin air.

Shine spun around, trying to see out the tiny rear door window. "Yo – wha' up?!"

Blow didn't answer. Didn't blink. Didn't move.

He threw the van in reverse – tires screeching, engine rattling – backing up just enough to angle the front end toward the next street over.

Shine's breathing picked up. "Man, wha' ya see?!"

Blow ignored him again, leaning so far forward his face was damn near pressed to the windshield. Then…

"Fuck!" He jammed the van into drive and punched the gas. The tires screamed, rubber streaking across the pavement.

Shine grabbed the back of the seat to steady himself. Again, he asked, "NIGGA, WHAT YOU SEE?!"

Still no answer. Instead, Blow fired back with his own question – loud, sharp. "Somebody follow y'all!?"

Roscoe shook his head immediately. "Not wha' ah seen."

"Me either," T-Man added.

Shine narrowed his eyes. "Man, WHAT THE HELL YOU SEEN?!"

Blow didn't answer – again. Instead, "Did ya scan da bags?"

Shine whipped his head toward Roscoe.

Roscoe swallowed. "Yeah," he said quickly. "I scanned dem all."

But Shine knew him. Knew how he lied. Knew how his voice got soft and his shoulders twitched.

Before Shine could press him, a police siren wailed close by. Too close.

Shine whipped around in time to see blue lights flicker through the buildings as Blow cut a sharp left.

"FUCK!" Shine hissed.

His nerves erupted. He stepped over the carts, digging through bags, tossing random tools aside.

"Where dat scanner at?!"

Roscoe patted himself down – hard, frantic – then stopped. His face dropped.

"Shit…" he whispered. "I… I think-I think ah lef' it in da jumpsuit pocket…"

Shine stared at him in disbelief. "NIGGA, HOW DA FU…"

The van halted again – Blow slamming the brakes. Everything became noise. Screeching tires. Sirens echoing off walls.

Shine's own heartbeat slamming in his ears.

"OUT! OUT! OUT!" Blow shouted.

Blow swerved the van at an angle blocking the street, forcing cruisers to swerve around it. The cops clipped a mailbox, skidded into each other – buying a few precious seconds. Shine, T-Man, and Roscoe had enough time to snatch the bags from the carts and bail before Blow took off, slinging the van down another street.

Carrying all six of the money bags, they took off running between two houses, feet pounding the dirt, breaths jagged in the humid Charleston air.

Shine's mind raced as they quickly sprinted through another back-yard and up a driveway. Up ahead, he saw a trashcan in another back-yard. Without thinking, he kicked it over, trash bursting across the ground. He snatched the black trash bag from the mess and tossed it open.

"Dump the fucking money in here!" Shine ordered.

Roscoe blinked at the money, guilt swirling in his eyes. Then, he looked at Shine.

"Look ya… it my fault," he said, voice low but steady. "I'ma lead 'em 'way from y'all. I gon' dump dem bank bags somewheh dey can find 'em."

Shine's eyes widened. "Man, we jus' gon' keep movin'. We good."

"Nah." Roscoe shook his head firmly. "Nah, bro. Dis on me. I ain' lettin' y'all crash behind my slip-up. You my nigga."

Roscoe grabbed Shine, pulled him into a quick, tight embrace – foreheads pressed against one another's for half a second. A lifetime of friendship in that one moment.

Then, just like that, Roscoe snatched the empty canvas bags and took off sprinting down the opposite street.

Shine took a step after him, mouth open, but T-Man grabbed his arm. "Let 'em go, yeh," he said quietly. "Let 'em go."

Shine swallowed hard – even though his throat felt tight as rope.

Then, the sirens hit again, closer than before, bouncing off every wall in the neighborhood. Shine and T-Man ducked behind a house then kept moving, their shadows racing alongside them as their lungs burned. The tension tightened around their necks like a noose.

The sun was high and blazing straight down on them like God was watching everything they weren't supposed to be doing.

Shine and T-Man continued to move soon as Roscoe disappeared into the maze of houses. The air was hot, heavy, buzzing with the sound of cicadas. Sweat trickled into Shine's eyes, but he didn't dare blink too long. His ears were tuned for sirens, for footsteps, for anything moving besides him and T-Man.

Behind them, sirens wailed from three different streets, overlapping like a warning. They weren't outrunning anybody.

The trash bag full of money slapped against Shine's thigh with every stride, slowing him just enough to remind him how real this was. How real the consequences were. How real Angela's face looked the last time he saw her breathing through those tubes.

He couldn't get caught. Not today. Not now.

T-Man grabbed Shine's arm and yanked him left between two more houses. A woman on the porch screamed as they sprinted past her, nearly knocking over her potted plants.

"MOVE, nigga!" T-Man barked, voice shredding his throat.

They hopped a wooden fence into a yard where two kids were playing with water guns. The kids froze, eyes going wide, their little mouths hanging open.

"Don' look at us!" Shine snapped, breath ragged. "Go inside!"

The kids scattered, dropping their toys.

They hit the next fence hard – very hard. The old wood cracked under their weight, sending Shine tumbling into the next yard. His shoulder popped painfully, but he forced himself back up before his mind could think about it. T-Man landed beside him, rolling to his feet like he'd been training all his life for this one moment.

"Dey gaining, bro," T-Man muttered. "I hear 'em."

Shine heard it too. The crunch of boots hitting gravel. The clacking of walkie-talkies. A cruiser turning a corner so fast that the tires screamed.

Another backyard. Another fence. Another desperate sprint through people's private lives as if the whole neighborhood was a maze built for only them to survive.

A dog barked loudly from behind a chain-link fence, throwing itself at them. T-Man grabbed Shine's collar and dragged him before the dog could get close enough to nip skin.

Shine's heart was beating so fast he thought it might explode.

He kept seeing Angela and her little hand in his. How light it had felt. How fragile. *I cain't get caught. Not today. Not 'fore she wake up.*

They cut through an alley behind a row of duplexes, their shadows stretching long in the bright afternoon sun.

Suddenly, a police cruiser skidded into the alley in front of them, blocking the way. The cop jumped out, reaching for his weapon.

"STOP! DON'T MOVE!" the officer screamed.

T-Man didn't hesitate; he shoved Shine into the side yard of another house.

They darted between more houses so close together Shine had to turn sideways to fit. The siding scraped his arms, the money bag clutched tight to his chest.

They popped out the other side into another open yard. A clothes-line hung low. Shine ducked under it; T-Man caught it with his neck and stumbled, but the last thing on his mind was stopping.

Another cruiser swung down the street, lights flashing. They were boxed in on three sides now.

"Go! Go! Through heah!" T-Man yelled, pointing to a narrow passage between two garage sheds.

It was barely wide enough for one person. The space was dark and packed with old junk – bikes, paint cans, tools, spiderwebs covering them like sheets. Shine shoved through it all, scraping his elbows as he ducked under a hanging rusted rake.

The sunlight hit his eyes again as they burst out the other end.

And then, Shine froze. Dead end. A chain-link fence that reached at least seven feet tall. Barbed wire was curled at the top with a slight opening parting it.

Behind it was freedom – a long, open field. But no way to cross over fast enough.

T-Man slammed into Shine's back, eyes going wide the moment he saw it. "Ah, fuck…" he breathed.

Sirens swung around the block to their right. They could hear the pounding of feet some yards behind them. Shadows grew long on the grass. They were cornered.

Shine grabbed the fence, shaking it like he could will it to fall.

"Climb it!" T-Man barked, climbing up enough to spread the opening in the barb wire farther apart for Shine.

Shine threw the money bag over the top – watched it tumble to the other side of the fence and hit the ground with a heavy thud. His arms were screaming, his lungs burning, his hands slick with sweat. He gripped the wire tight and hauled himself upward. His shoes slipped twice before he finally managed to hook a leg over.

Sweat burned his eyes. His whole body felt like jelly. He could hear the cops closing in – shouts, radios, footsteps slamming against the earth.

He swung his legs over the other side, landing hard on concrete. The pistol tumbled from his waistline as pain shot up his ankle, but he didn't stop. He scooped up the trash bag full of money and the gun then turned back toward the fence.

"T-Man! Come on, yeh!" Shine hissed, tucking the pistol before reaching up to pull at the barb wire like T-Man had just done for him.

But T-Man wasn't climbing. He stood on the other side, chest heaving, hands trembling – not from fear but from a decision.

There was a look in his eyes Shine had only seen a handful of times

– the look of a man who had already made his peace with a particular situation.

"T-Man… wha' da hell ya doin'?" Shine growled, voice cracking.

T-Man didn't answer at first. He glanced over his shoulder. Police echoes were getting louder from the front of the home. They were getting closer. The fence trembled from the pressure of Shine gripping it, begging without words.

Finally, T-Man turned fully toward Shine, jaw clenched.

"Bro… go on," he said quietly, nodding toward the right side of the yard. "Ah'ma take dey ass down dis way."

Shine froze. His stomach dropped. "Nah… hell noh. Come on, bra!" Shine pleaded, pulling the fence like he could rip it open with his bare hands.

But T-Man shook his head. "Shine," he said in a calm, steady tone that didn't fit the chaos pounding around them, "Angela needs ya mo' than I do."

"T-Man…"

"GO!" T-Man barked – loud enough to snap Shine's soul in half.

Then, T-Man ran. He sprinted toward the opposite end of the yard – away from Shine, toward the cops. He made himself seen on purpose, slapping the side of a shed to draw their attention.

"Fuck y'all!" he shouted. "Y'all bitches gots ta catch me!"

Boots thundered after him instantly.

"T!" Shine choked out, gripping the fence until his knuckles whitened. But T-Man didn't turn back. He never did when he made up his mind.

Shine was forced to move. He backed away from the fence reluctantly, chest tight. He held tears he refused to let fall which began to sting his eyes. He turned and ran.

Shine ran through the tall grass, and through another yard, then over a shorter fence that cut his forearms on the way down. His breath was sharp, ragged, every inhale scraping like glass. The trash bag slapped his leg as he sprinted through stranger's worlds – garden hoses, bikes, toys scattered across lawns.

Every siren sounded like it was right behind him.

The sunlight made it worse. There was nowhere to hide, nowhere to blend in. He was exposed, hunted.

He cut through an alley, ducked behind a shed, slipped between two garbage cans that were so close and tight that he had to turn sideways to squeeze between. His lungs were screaming. His legs were on fire. His mind kept flashing with one picture. T-Man running the other way, leading the cops off. T-Man… maybe was dying for him.

"Fuck," Shine gasped under his breath, pushing harder.

He jumped a ditch, nearly fell, but kept running. Voices yelled behind him; he couldn't tell how close they were.

Then suddenly, the alley spit him out into a busy street.

Cars honked. People walked on the sidewalks. Traffic lights blinked. A transit bus was rolling up to a stop across the five lane street with its air brakes hissing.

Shine didn't think, nor did he plan. Instinct took over. He sprinted across the street, dodging cars. A horn blared inches from him.

A few people waiting at the bus stop turned their heads. There was a chubby girl standing at the very end, AirPods in her ears. She held her phone like she was texting.

Shine skidded up to her so fast she jumped.

"Wha' the…"

Shine ripped a hundred-dollar bill from the stack of money inside the bag and shoved it toward her.

"Pay my fee!" he gasped. "An' ya keep da rest!"

She stared at him, confused, mouth open like she didn't know whether to scream or run. But then the sirens echoed down the block – loud, closing in.

Her eyes widened. "Uh… shit…" She snatched the bill.

Shine slipped in behind her just as the doors hissed open. She slid a few bills into the reader and waved him through.

The bus driver squinted at Shine, taking in his torn clothes, sweat, and wild eyes.

"Ya good?" the driver asked.

"Yeh," Shine panted.

The doors closed.

A police cruiser turned onto the street just as the bus pulled off. Another cruiser shot through the intersection from the opposite side. The bus glided between them, traffic swallowing their view for a precious few seconds.

Shine collapsed into the very last seat, the bag of money gripped in his lap like a newborn. Sweat dripped down his face onto the trash bag.

His heartbeat was so loud he could hear it echoing through the bus seats.

He didn't look outside. He didn't look up. All he saw in his mind was T-Man… running the other way, and Shine had no idea if his brother was dead or alive.

But the bus kept moving. And Shine – broken, shaking, terrified – was still free.

CHAPTER FOURTEEN

The bus hissed as it slowed to a stop, and Shine yanked the cord like it burned his fingers. His whole body felt heavy when he stood – clothes stiff with sweat, dust, and the long day that had almost halted his seventeen years on this earth. His legs wobbled like they were remembering every sprint, every alley, every close call.

When he stepped down onto the pavement, the Charleston heat hit him again, thick and swampy. The sun was low now, dipping behind the skyline, casting the streets in that burnt-orange haze that made everything look worn out… like the whole city was tired right along with him.

Shine stepped off, landing on shaky legs. Every step toward Big Mo's studio felt like walking through someone else's life. Cars rolled by in slow traffic, people laughed on the sidewalks, a whole world was going on like nothing had happened. Like T-Man wasn't bleeding on a patch of dirt somewhere. Like Shine hadn't just robbed a Wells Fargo for his sister's chance at living.

The studio sat wedged between a barbershop and a vegan café, the neon sign buzzing faintly above his head. He took a breath, wiped his palms on his filthy catering uniform, then hit the call button. He lifted his chin to the camera, everybody had to, letting them get a clean look at the dirt smeared across his face, the torn sleeve, the black plastic bag clenched in his fist.

The long buzz sounded. The lock clicked.

Shine stepped inside. KG was standing right there in the hallway like he'd been waiting for him. His eyebrow lifted damn near to his hairline when he saw Shine.

"Boi," KG said slowly, eyes running over his clothes, the scratches on his arms, the bag he wouldn't let go of, "ya don' found a new job… ain't you?"

Shine forced a short breath through his nose. "Somethin' like dat. Big Mo in da back?"

KG didn't say a word. He just stared a second longer – like he knew what was going on – but finally nodded and stepped aside. Shine walked past him, every footstep echoing louder in his head than in the actual hallway.

He reached Mo's office door, knocked once, then turned the handle.

Big Mo was hunched over paperwork, the diamond rings on his finger clicking to the rhythm of his fingers. When he looked up, his whole face lit up in that familiar half-smile.

"My lil nigga, Shine," Mo greeted, leaning back in his chair. "How ya holdin' up, baby boi?"

But the smile faded the moment he really looked at him – looked at the grime, the torn uniform, the bruised arms, the swollen lip. Then, his eyes dropped to the black trash bag.

Shine sat down without waiting to be told. "Can ya still write that check out fo' me?"

Mo's eyebrow arched. "That wha' you got in the bag?"

Shine gave a short and tight nod.

Mo blinked once then slowly leaned back. His lips twisted as he looked toward the ceiling, like a thought had clicked.

"So, dat was you an' ya people tear'n through King Street earliah?"

Shine didn't answer. Didn't even blink.

Mo studied him hard. "Shine…"

"Can ya help me or no?" Shine cut him off, voice flat and almost empty. He didn't have anything left to give to this moment except desperation.

Silence filled the room, thick enough to choke on.

Mo didn't move nor say anything at first. He just stared at Shine like he was seeing two versions of him – the scared little kid who used to hang around the studio and the grown man who just walked in with blood on his soul.

Shine's thoughts began to spiral. By now, every news station had to be plastering grainy footage of the robbery everywhere. The Wells Fargo heist. Suspects on foot. One believed to still be at large.

The money in that bag was burning a hole straight to prison. If Mo didn't help him, there was no legal way to hand over cash like this to a doctor. Angela's treatment depended on somebody taking a chance on him… and Big Mo was that somebody.

He stared back at Mo, jaw tight, heart pounding so hard it hurt.

If Angela died… then what was his life even worth?

His hand brushed the pistol tucked at his side – not a threat, not even a thought until now… just a reminder that he was past the point of no return.

Finally, Big Mo let out a long breath through his nose.

"I got ya…" he said quietly.

The words hit Shine so hard his shoulders instantly dropped into a sag. Relief washed through him so sharp it almost made him dizzy.

But Mo wasn't finished. He rubbed his hands together, leaning forward with a weighty seriousness. "I got ya… but it come at a cost you prob'ly can afford. Not to mention how hot that paper is."

Shine heard him, but his body wasn't listening. Inside, something had cracked open – something he'd been holding shut to keep himself functioning. His breath shook when he let it out. His head dropped. His eyes blurred with the kind of gratefulness that didn't fit inside words.

He didn't know how much cash was actually in the bag. But he knew they pulled two extra bags from the truck. Whatever Mo wanted, whatever he charged – he could cover it. It didn't matter because Angela would live.

At that moment, he wanted to say a thousand things to Mo. Wanted to tell him about T-Man. About running for his life. About the fear, the guilt, the hope. He wanted to tell him thank you in a way that fit the size of the miracle he'd just been handed.

But all he could feel was the raw truth pulling at his chest. If Angela wasn't here, none of this mattered. The running, the fear, the near-death moments… empty without her. And because Mo had looked him in the eye and said, *"I got ya,"* his little sister finally had a shot at staying in this world.

Shine swallowed hard, forcing his voice steady.

He didn't say it out loud. But he knew he'd never forget this.

CHAPTER FIFTEEN

Weeks Later

Shine sat back in the hard plastic chair, one leg stretched out, the other bouncing slow from nerves he didn't want his mama to see.

The surgery, according to the doctor, had went well. They had done the job, and now him and his mother had been patiently waiting for the light of their world to return home.

A winter sun pushed through the hospital blinds in pale, weak stripes, settling across Angela's blanket like a blessing too small to matter, but somehow it was still enough. The room smelled like soap, hand sanitizer, and the kind of quiet sadness hospitals always carried, the kind most folks never got used to – the kind Shine had learned to live with.

But it was Christmas, and Christmas had a way of rewriting the room.

He leaned his head back against the wall and let his mind drift where it wanted – back to that day on the calendar that came around no matter who was sick, broke, hurting, or missing. Christmas didn't care. It rolled through with its lights and songs and fake snow and peppermint smells, carrying a joy the world sometimes didn't deserve.

Christmas, Shine thought, staring at the blinking machine beside his sister's bed, *ain't nuthin' but ah date — but look how it changes errything.*

He thought about how it landed on different days of the week each year – Monday, Wednesday, Saturday… didn't matter. Once December 25th hit, the air felt different. People got kinder – or at least pretended to be. Kids woke up early. Stoves stayed hot. Houses smelled like cinnamon and baked ham. Even the streets felt softer.

When he was small, Christmas used to be magic. Pure and easy magic.

He let a soft smile tug the corner of his mouth as a memory washed over him.

He and Angela – back when she was tiny with chubby cheeks and wild braids – used to run to the Christmas tree before the sun even thought about rising. Their mama used to yell, "Y'all betta not wake me before six," but they never listened. The excitement was too loud in their bodies.

Shine remembered tearing wrapping paper like it owed him money, ripping bows off boxes, and Angela squealing every time she found something pink. She'd clap her little hands, eyes bright as Christmas lights.

And there was her smile… Lord, her smile.

There were winters when money was tight – tight like a fist – and Christmas was thin. Some years, their presents were dollar store toys. One year, the tree was nothing but three branches and a prayer. But Angela's baby smile made every broke Christmas look rich.

Dat smile, Shine thought, swallowing the knot rising in his chest, *was always 'nough fo' me. Always.*

He blinked slow, bringing himself back to the hospital room where the machines hummed and his mama sat beside Angela, gently brushing her hair back from her forehead. Mama's hands were tired hands – hands that had scrubbed floors, packed lunches, wiped tears, fought life back every time it tried taking something from them.

Shine opened his mouth to speak, but before he could, Angela's eyelids fluttered.

His heart stopped.

"Baby?" Mama whispered, leaning forward.

Angela's eyelids fluttered again, slower this time, like whatever strength she had was choosing carefully how to return to her. Her fingers twitched under the blanket – small, almost invisible movements – but Shine felt each one like a shock straight to the heart. He leaned forward, elbows on his knees, breath held without meaning to.

Then her eyes opened fully.

Soft brown eyes that didn't shine the way they used to, not yet – but they were still hers. Still the same eyes that used to follow him around the living room on Christmas morning, the same eyes that lit up when he stole her extra peppermints from church, the same eyes that begged him to braid her doll's hair even though he never got the parts straight.

And when those eyes focused on him, really focused, her lips tugged up into a tiny, tired smile.

Not the big, gummy grin she used to rock as a kid. Not the full-toothed, unstoppable one she gave when she danced around the kitchen.

But a small, trembling smile she fought for through weakness and pain. A smile that cost her something.

A smile she still gave him anyway.

Shine's throat tightened so hard he had to look down for a second. Angela always smiled for him – even when she was hurting, even when she was scared, even when she was trying to be brave because she didn't want him crying.

He remembered a night three months back – her worst night. She had been curled up, shaking from the pain, her tiny body exhausted from vomiting from some minor sickness. He'd sat on the edge of her bed, rubbing her back in slow circles, feeling useless. Angela could barely lift her head, but she whispered, "Don' cry, Shine… It jes ah little bad day."

He cried anyway – quietly. Shine remember having to face the wall, yet she had still seen him.

That same girl – his baby sister who always tried to protect him – was now lying under a blanket too big for her, hooked to machines too cold for her. Still giving him a smile she should've saved for her own strength.

Her hand rose weakly off the bed, fingers curled like she was reaching through water. Shine caught it gently, terrified of squeezing too hard and hurting her.

"Hey, big brotha…" she whispered, voice rough like she hadn't used it in two lifetimes.

It broke him.

He nodded because speaking would've made him crumble in front of her. His jaw clenched until it trembled. His eyes burned. He swallowed his pain, swallowed his fear, swallowed everything she didn't need to see – because for once, he had to be the strong one.

Mama leaned in too, brushing back Angela's hair, her touch slow and careful. Angela leaned into it like she hadn't felt softness in days.

"Ya scared us, baby," Mama whispered, voice thick. "Ya almost give me a heart attack."

Angela blinked, a slow blink filled with apology she shouldn't have to carry. Then she turned her head, just enough to look at Shine again.

"I knew… I was sleep," she breathed out, voice thin as paper. "I saw Daddy."

Shine bowed his head into their joined hands. That was his undoing because she wasn't lying.

His mind flashed to every night he'd begged God – quietly, angrily, desperately – not to take her. Every deal he'd tried to make in his head. Every moment of panic when she wouldn't wake up. Every time he walked into that hospital room wondering if he was about to lose the one soul that never judged him, never doubted him, never called him a disappointment.

Angela squeezed his hand – weak pressure, barely there – but to Shine, it felt like a lifeline.

"Then I dreamed… you were singing, then ya left," she murmured. "I didn't want ta be alone. That's why I wake up."

Shine's breath caught. He was glad that she didn't know.

She had no idea how much he had done for her. What he had survived and had almost lost. He had stolen and risked it all for her

All for a chance – just a chance – to see her open her eyes again.

He squeezed back, tears gathering at the edges of his eyes but never falling. Not yet. Not in front of her.

"I right heah, Angie," he whispered, voice hoarse. "I ain' gon' nowhere."

Her smile widened, the kind of smile you get once in a lifetime. The kind of smile that changed a man into a child.

Angela held onto his arm, resting her small hand against his sleeve like she was making sure he wasn't a dream. She studied his face, the worry lines, the exhaustion he couldn't hide.

"You look tired," she whispered. "Did ya… have a rough night?"

Shine almost laughed at how simple she said it. *A rough night. Ya could say dat.*

But he shook his head. "No. I alright now."

And he meant it because she was breathing. She was awake.

Everything else – the robbery, the police chase, the close calls, the blood, the guilt – none of it mattered next to her heartbeat.

Angela blinked slow again, but not from exhaustion this time. From comfort. From peace. Like waking up wasn't just a medical moment but a miracle she was easing herself into.

"Can I… have the curtain open?" she asked. "I wan' see… wha' day it is."

Mama stood to pull the blinds open, letting in a stronger light. White and gold spilled across Angela's face, making her look angelic and fragile and unbelievably alive all at once.

"It Christmas," Shine said softly.

Angela's lips parted, wonder washing over her. "Oh…" she breathed. "I made it ta Christmas."

Shine brushed his knuckle against her cheek, careful and reverent. "Yeh," he whispered, voice cracking. "Ya made it."

Her eyes filled, but not from pain. From relief and gratitude.

She wasn't a miracle. She was proof a miracle could happen. And for Shine… that was enough to save his whole world. That smile was the only present he wanted this year. Hell, it was the only one he'd wanted last year too.

He held onto it for a moment, letting it soak deep before his thoughts drifted – because truth had a way of coming back, even during blessings.

He shifted for a few moments to things that made this possible. Blow.

Crazy-ass Blow, who had decided he could drive a van like he was in a *Fast & Furious* movie. Shine shook his head, laughing under his breath despite himself. Blow hit that corner during the robbery getaway like the laws of physics only applied to other people.

The boi crashed dat van into a pole so hard, Shine thought, *da airbags jumped out first an' apologized.*

Blow got caught right there, slumped over the wheel, glass and pieces of metal scattered everywhere like confetti. Caught red-handed.

He ended up with eight years. He was lucky it wasn't more.

Then, Shine thought about Roscoe. *Lawd have mercy.*

Roscoe ran when the police showed up – ran like he had Olympic scouts watching. But what he didn't know was that Charleston PD had pulled up with a whole K-9 unit.

The dog had come around the corner like it had a personal vendetta.

Roscoe hollered, "I GIVE UP!" But his legs didn't match his mouth because the man kept running. The dog chased him across a yard, over a kiddie pool, through a hedge, and tackled him dead into somebody's inflatable Santa Claus.

Neighbors were taking videos. Kids were cheering.

Somebody yelled, "Git 'em, Rudolph!" even though it wasn't even a reindeer.

Roscoe ended up with bite marks, a sprained ankle, and five years. And a bit of humiliation.

Then Shine's mind shifted to T-Man, and the humor drained from his chest.

T-Man… His heart twisted.

He could envision the moment – could almost hear the gunshots – could see T-Man throw his hands up, surrendering, giving up because he didn't want Shine to die out there. He imagined watching the cops shoot him anyway, hitting him so hard his body folded before he even hit the ground.

Shine clenched his jaw until it hurt.

The city had tried to bury it – tried to twist the story. But Angela wasn't the only fighter in that hospital. T-Man, through pain and anger and a lawyer who didn't play about the injustice, pushed hard. Claimed unlawful force. Showed proof and got the right support.

The city settled that lawsuit quietly in a back office somewhere – an amount T-Man never bragged about. They gave him a felony and misdemeanor, a joke of a charge, then ushered him out the back door of the courtroom like they wanted him forgotten.

But Shine would never forget. T-Man had taken a bullet for him, almost lost his life for him. However, he'd lost the normal life he should've had.

Then the memory shifted again – to the thing Shine kept tucked away in the dark corners of his mind.

The fourth man. The one who dipped before anyone could see his face.

The very same one the news kept calling, "the unidentified suspect." The one the police said was still at large.

Still wanted and out there.

Shine didn't know if that man was alive, gone, or watching from somewhere far. It didn't matter. His name was inked on the page of that day forever.

He looked over at his mother – her eyes soft, tired, but proud in a way he hadn't seen in years. She rested her hand on Angela's foot, rubbing it gently through the blanket.

Then Angela looked at him with her sleepy smile, the one that cracked his whole world open.

Shine breathed out slow. "I love y'all," he whispered.

His mama smiled back, wiping a tear. Angela reached out her hand, fingers weak but determined, and Shine took it gently.

He let the moment sit – warm, peaceful, real – before his mind moved one last time to something lighter, something he hadn't expected to matter so much.

His track that night at The Pad – when him and T-man performed in front of a crowd for the first time – the DJ had kept the song after Shine walked out the club. Something about the pain in Shine's voice, the grit, the truth – it grabbed the room. And the DJ played it again the next night. And the night after.

Shine didn't even know that people were now requesting it. Shouting it out. Recording and sharing it.

The track crawled out of Charleston, crossed South Carolina lines, and started popping up in Atlanta, Charlotte, Jacksonville… and then farther.

By the time Shine walked back into Big Mo's studio after Angela woke up, Mo was pacing around with his phone in his hand like he was about to propose to somebody.

Labels were now calling. Numbers were being mentioned. Real numbers. Numbers Shine could finally understand.

Mo kept saying things like, "Look ya, Shine… I tell you – dey want ya. But da industry crooked, boi. Dese labels smell blood in the water. Ya betta move smart. Real smart."

Shine didn't know much about corporate tricks or contracts or percentages, but he knew one thing. His voice was finally worth something.

And more importantly…

It could take care of Angela the right way. Forever.

He looked back at his mama. At Angela. At the sunlight sliding across their faces. He felt something inside him settle – a heavy chapter finally closing.

Christmas. Family.

T-Man was still breathing. Angela was smiling again. His music was rising. And the future – uncertain but finally possible.

Shine leaned back in the chair and closed his eyes, letting the warmth of the moment wash over him.

Life wasn't fair. Never had been. But right now?

Right now, life was giving him a small piece of peace. And Shine was determined to hold onto it with both hands.

The End

DID YOU ENJOY?

Did you enjoy the read?
Let us know how much by leaving us a
review on Amazon and Goodreads.

OTHER BOOKS BY
Urban Aint Dead

Tales 4rm Da Dale

The Hottest Summer Ever

Hittin' Licks For The Holidays: Atlanta

Wet Dreams On Lockdown: The Nurse

How To Publish A Book From Prison

How To Invest In The Stock Market From Prison

First Summer Out With My Prison Bae

By **Elijah R. Freeman**

Despite The Odds

Despite The Odds 2

By **Juhnell Morgan**

Hittaz

Hittaz 2

Hittaz 3

Hittaz 4

Hittaz 5

Hittaz 6

Coldhearted

Coldhearted 2

Coldhearted 3

By **Lou Garden Price, Sr.**

A YN'S Muse For The Summer

Wizdom: Forever Your Gangsta

Charge It To The Game

Charge It To The Game 2

Charge It To The Game 3

A Summer To Remember With My Hitta

Snatched Up By A Hitta

Santa Sent Me A Real One For Christmas

Wet Dreams On Lockdown: The Unit Manager

Thug Me The Right Way 2

Thug Me The Right Way 3

Seizing A Gangsta's Heart For The Summer

Yours For The Taking

Wrapped Up In A Hitta's Love For Christmas

By **Nai**

A Set Up For Revenge

A Set Up For Revenge 2

Wet Dreams On Lockdown: The Librarian

By **Ashley Williams**

Trickin' On A Heaux For Christmas

Homie Hoppin' For The Holidays

Wet Dreams On Lockdown: The Female C.O

Letters Of His Love

By **Telia Teanna**

The State's Witness

The State's Witness 2

The State's Witness 3

This Time Won't You Save Me

This Time Won't You Save Me 2

His Summer Side Piece

A Holiday Heist

Healing The Heart Of A Detroit Gangsta

Summer Vows With A Detroit Gangsta

The Promissory

The Promissory 2

A Gangsta's Last Kiss

By **Kyiris Ashley**

Stuck In The Trenches

Stuck In The Trenches 2

By **Huff Tha Great**

Melted The Heart Of A Menace

Wet Dreams On Lockdown: Lieutenant Grace

By **P. Wise**

Merry Trapmas

By **Mia Sky**

Thug Me The Right Way

By **DiamondATL & Nai**

Wet Dreams On Lockdown: The Counselor

By **Paris Iman**

Wet Dreams On Lockdown: The Male C.O

By **Tamyra Griffin**

Wet Dreams On Lockdown: The Captain

By **TN Jones**

Wet Dreams On Lockdown: The Warden

By **Shawnice**

Coming Soon From
URBAN AINT DEAD

Drill
The Hottest Summer Ever 2
THE G-CODE
Tales 4rm Da Dale 2
How To Build Your Credit From Prison
By **Elijah R. Freeman**

Despite The Odds 3
By **Juhnell Morgan**

A Hitman's Gift For Christmas
A Felon's Promise
By **Nai**

What Do The Lonely Do At Christmas
By Kyiris Ashley

To Die For
By **Tron Hill**

Bandemic 3
By Freshh Moneyy

ASSISTED PUBLISHING PACKAGES

Bronze Package

- Includes:
    - Cover Design
    - Editing
    - Formatting/Typesetting
    - Publishing Consultation
    - Price: $400

Silver Package

- Includes:
    - Cover Design
    - Typing
    - Editing
    - One Flyer
    - Formatting/Typesetting
    - Publishing Consultation
    - Price: $725

Gold Package

- Includes:
- Cover Design
- Typing
- Editing
- Proofreading
- Two Flyers
- Formatting/Typesetting
- Copyright Registration
- Publishing Consultation
- Amazon Upload
  - Price: $975

Platinum Package

- Includes:
- All-in-One Bundle: Typing, Editing, Proofreading, Formatting/Typesetting
- Cover Design
- Three Flyers
- Publishing Consultation
- Copyright Registration
- Amazon Setup & Upload
- One Month Promotion
- Amazon Setup/ Upload
  - Price: $1,200

Individual Services

1.Editing Services
- •Proofreading: $100
- •Manuscript Editing:
- •0-60k words: $350
- •Contact for a quote for manuscripts over 60k words.

2.Manuscript Preparation

•Formatting/Typesetting: We will prepare and arrange your book's text and interior for printing.
   •Price: $100

3.Design Services
   •Cover Design: $100 (2 free revisions, any additional revisions will be an additional cost)
   •Promo Flyer: $25
   •Custom Flyer: Contact for quote

4.Distribution Services
   •Amazon KDP Setup: $25
   •Amazon Upload: $25 (if you already have an account but just need us to upload it for you)

5.Other Services
   •Typing: $300 for manuscripts up to 40k words (Contact for quote for longer projects).

   •Copyright Registration: $100 + site registration fees.

U.A.D PROMOTION PACKAGES

Tier 1: The Basics Package

Price: $99

Target Audience: First-time or budget-conscious authors seeking minimal exposure.

Perks:

- Social Media Shoutout: 3 IG Story posts a week for a month.
  - Inclusion in Newsletter: Mention in the "Sponsored Showcase" section with a link to the book.
  - Digital Promo Graphic: A simple branded image featuring the book cover for the author's use (i.e. Available Now flyer)
  - Support Sunday Link In U.A.D FB Group: Book cover and link in Support Sunday post in group (x4)

Tier 2: The Spotlight Package

Price: $199

Target Audience: Authors seeking increased visibility for their release.

Perks:

- Social Media Shoutout: 3 IG Story posts a week for a month.
  - Inclusion in Newsletter: Mention in the "Sponsored Showcase" section with a link to the book.
  - Digital Promo Graphic: A simple branded image featuring the book cover for the author's use (i.e. Available Now flyer)
  - Support Sunday Link In U.A.D FB Group: Book cover and link in Support Sunday post in group (x4)
  - FB Group Promo: Book posted Monday-Friday in over 20 Urban Reader FB Groups for a month.

<u>Tier 3: Maximum Visibility Package</u>

Price: $299

Target Audience: Authors seeking an increased promotional push.

Perks:

- Social Media Shoutout: 3 IG Story posts a week for a month.
  - Inclusion in Newsletter: Mention in the "Sponsored Showcase" section with a link to the book.
  - Digital Promo Graphic: A simple branded image featuring the book cover for the author's use (i.e. Available Now flyer)
  - Custom Quote Graphic: 3 Eye Catching Quote Graphics that can be used on Social Media.

- 3 To 5 Character Visuals: Visuals of the characters in your book that can be used for promo.
- Support Sunday Link In U.A.D FB Group: Book cover and link in Support Sunday post in group (x4)
- FB Group Promo: Book posted Monday-Friday in over 20 Urban Reader FB Groups for a month.
- Paid Ad: We will run an Ad for your book for a month on a Sponsored Showcase page with a customized caption, targeting your book's audience to grow your readership.

BOOKS BY

URBAN AINT DEAD's C.E.O

<u>Elijah R. Freeman</u>

Triggadale 1, 2 & 3

Tales 4rm Da Dale

The Hottest Summer Ever

Murda Was The Case 1, 2 & 3

Hittin' Licks For The Holidays: Atlanta

Wet Dreams On Lockdown: The Nurse

How To Publish A Book From Prison

How To Invest In The Stock Market From Prison

STAY CONNECTED

Follow
Elijah R. Freeman
On Social Media

FB: Elijah R. Freeman
IG: @the_future_of_urban_fiction